A ROYAL CHRISTMAS CRUISE

A STONEWALL INVESTIGATIONS- MIAMI HOLIDAY STORY

MAX WALKER

Edited By: ONE LOVE EDITING

Proofread By: Tanja Ongkiehong

Cover Design: Max Walker

Copyright © 2019 by Max Walker

All rights reserved.

SYNOPSIS

Nicholas Silva

This Christmas, I was determined to change things.

I was done living a lie. I felt like a puppet, so I cut the strings. I woke up one morning and parted ways with my girlfriend - to the shock of everyone. That same day, I had tickets booked on a holiday cruise where I planned on cutting loose and finding the truth I had been denying myself all along.

Little did I know, I would end up finding what I was looking for in the jaw-droppingly handsome man I met before boarding the ship. Our chemistry was immediate, and it wasn't long before we shared a passionate kiss.

Then came his question. He asked me to be fake boyfriends with him for the duration of the cruise.

My immediate urge was to say 'yes' except for a tiny complication that forced me to reconsider: I'm the prince of Spain and I am still very much closeted.

Shiro Brooks

This Christmas was supposed to be for reuniting with old friends. I didn't expect to be dealing with a break-up and becoming the seventh wheel. I tried staying positive, but after an embarrassing situation at the security checkpoint, I resigned myself to my crummy holiday fate.

Imagine my Santa-sized surprise when I bump into (and subsequently make-out with) the hottest man I'd ever met in my entire life. Drunk off our connection, I blurt out a crazy proposal.

A proposal that he instantly shoots down.

I for sure thought it would all end there. I had no idea it was only just the beginning of our story.

1 NICHOLAS SILVA

The kisses came at me like mosquitos fighting to get through a protective net. Fast, sharp, unwelcome.

Her lips pecked at my neck first. Like she was searching for some sort of weak spot, where she could break skin and suck out my blood. I wondered briefly if I should let her. Just succumb to the blood-draining, like I'd succumbed to being in this fraud of a relationship for two years now.

All so Papi and Mami could live happy, knowing their little prince was finding himself a queen.

I rolled onto my side, cutting off the kisses. She huffed a breath of air before I felt the bed tremble as she fell back on it. I kept my eyes trained forward, on my chipped dresser, set so that it blocked half of the window, keeping the dusty red curtain permanently closed.

I hated the view. It reminded me of a prison. Keeping it

shut meant I could lie on my bed without having to look out at the constant reminder of my, eh, situation. The only reason I even knew it was midday was because the sunlight barreled through the unblocked side of the window, throwing half my room into light and the other into shadow.

"What's going on Nick? ¿Que pasa?"

The question didn't come out of the blue. Cristella was a very caring, very empathetic woman, which made this situation all the more difficult. She was a proper girl, and a beautiful one, I'd admit. I've come to learn that she wasn't my type in the slightest, but her beauty could never be denied.

I rolled over, facing her, looking into those doe-like green eyes, some of the waves of her silky brown hair cresting across her forehead, hiding a couple of freckles that dotted her flawless skin. Her pouty lips looked extra pouty. Normally, I would kiss her until I got a smile. I had always felt like that's what I was supposed to do, how I was supposed to act. So I had.

But not today. Not after this morning. There would be no more kisses.

"You're scaring me." Her eyes bounced between mine. "You're scaring a lot of us. You've just been in your room, for hours. Days. You missed the dinner yesterday, and you missed the fund-raising lunch last weekend. That was one of your favorite events of the entire year. And you wouldn't even tell me why..."

Because I can't look into anyone's eyes anymore, not without thinking I'm a fucking fraud.

"I haven't been feeling well," I answered, giving my default response to any similar questions hurled my way over the past couple of months. Cristella wasn't the only one who could pick up on my shift in attitude. Both my parents had briefly brought it up over dinner about two weeks ago. The conversation lasted approximately three minutes before my dad began talking about the preparations for the Christmas festival.

"But why?" Cristella had determination in her eyes. She wasn't letting this go for idle chat over holiday decorations. "What's going on in that head of yours?"

"A storm," I said, being honest for once in what felt like months. "I can't even pull out a single thought."

"Try. For me."

The thunderclouds filling my head exploded with lightning.

"That's the thing, Cristella... I need to do the opposite. I have to try for myself now."

"What are you talking about?"

I stared at the beauty mark that dotted her skin near the dip of her Cupid's bow. "I've been living for what everyone else wanted of me. The prince, an heir to a throne that doesn't even hold any power anymore. It's all just dressing on a set. People fall for it because it glitters under the light, but when the lights turn off, it all gets dark just like everything else. I've been living a lie for what? To make my parents happy? To keep the tabloids quiet?"

Cristella's eyes were filling with worry. A crease appeared between her thin brows. She started fiddling with her earlobe, something she always did when she became anxious.

"Don't talk about your family like that."

She didn't get it. They weren't family. They were prison

guards, keeping my true self stuffed deep down inside the darkest dungeon imaginable. Somewhere devoid of any kind of light.

Not anymore, though. Not anymore.

"I can't keep this in." I sat up in bed, leaning back on the plush bedframe, the soft white pleated velvet caressing my bare back.

"Keep what in? What are you talking about, Nicholas?"

I wanted to shout it then. Wanted even the guards standing outside the palace gates to hear me.

The words almost fell from me, but they hit a barricade somewhere in my chest. I stopped myself. Breaking up with my girlfriend would cause big enough waves. Was I ready to proclaim why I had broken up with her? Was I ready to tell everyone that I was gay?

No. The answer, right then and there, was no.

I mulled over my thoughts, warding away the fears that nipped at my heels like hungry wolves.

"What happened, Nick? Everything was fine this morning. We had a beautiful breakfast and a great chat over coffee. You seemed so optimistic. Happy, even. And then you go for a walk to Hightower Bridge, and the moment you get back, you act totally different. What happened to you on that walk?"

Everything happened. Nothing happened.

There was no way I could dive into that right now. I could only skate above it. Briefly.

"I realized some things this morning. Things I'd been thinking about a lot."

"And?"

"One of those things is..." I had to word this exactly

right. I hadn't prepared for this at all. "I don't think I'm right for you. I've realized this isn't going to work."

Shock seemed to have slapped her across the face. A rabbit-like sound slipped from her lips, like a frightened animal meeting its certain end.

"I'm sorry," I offered, as if that would somehow soothe the gaping wound on her heart. A wound I was sure grew larger by the second, by every accelerated thump.

Cristella was right in saying that this morning had been great. I woke up feeling better than I had felt in a long while, and that all might have been because of a dream I had woken up from, one that still lingered on my thoughts throughout the day, phantom kisses lingering on my lips.

It hadn't been a dream of me and Cristella, or of me and Angelina Jolie, or any other woman for that matter.

The dream, painted in technicolor bold and still replaying in my head, had me rolling across an infinite meadow of brightly colored poppies and daisies and sunflowers and lavender, their petals all throwing off rays of rainbow light as our two naked bodies writhed and our moans rose up to color the skies, which were dashes of pink and blue and orange and purple. Soon, the meadow of flowers disappeared, and the two of us were resting on a private island, golden sand glittering underneath us, slipping between our toes and our fingers as we moved into new positions, fucking and stroking and kissing.

I never remembered dreaming in such vivid color. Never.

Me and the man spent a night more passionate than I had spent with Cristella in the two years we'd been together. This dream had felt more real to me than any of the empty nights I had gone through the motions just to have sex with my own girlfriend.

And so yes, I *was* happy during our breakfast, but as Cristella cheerily listed out all the things she wanted to do in America for our holiday trip, I knew that my heart was somewhere far, far from the table. I wasn't happy because of her, not at all.

At the same time I couldn't be fully honest with her. If I told her I was breaking up with her because I was gay, then one: I'd always remember my first time coming out as something terrible, and two: it would be front-page news within the hour. I didn't want to risk that. I had to beat around the bush without beating up her heart too badly in the process. I still cared about her as a friend, and even though all throughout university I'd been rumored to be an overly cocky and heartbreaking *guapo* by the Spanish papers, an image that ended up sticking, in reality that portrayal of me wasn't true at all. I cared deeply about the people in my life, even if very few of them seemed to care much about me.

"How? Why?" Cristella said, her upper lip beginning to shake.

Cristella Montenegro, the only girl who had broken through the protective bubble I'd put up, and actually lasted as my girlfriend for longer than six months. Mainly because she had been forcibly pushed past it by my parents, who saw their young prince growing up without ever having one stable relationship, without ever finding his queen.

"Did I do something?" she continued. "*¿Que hice?*"

"You did nothing," I said, once again finding an opportunity to be absolutely truthful. "It has nothing to do with you."

"So what exactly are you saying?"

"I'm saying I can't be in this relationship anymore, Cristella. I just can't."

She shook her head, wiped at her cheeks. The skin around her neck and over her chest flushed bright red. She got up from the bed and walked over to the window, her steps soft on the floor and still somehow sounding like bombs going off in the silent room. She pushed aside the dresser with a surprising show of force. Her silk nightgown, light pink and hemmed in black, clung to her skin, hugging her hip bones as she whipped around and grabbed the thick red window blind.

"Cristella?"

"I need to see you. Need to see your face." She yanked the blind open, sunlight breaking in through the rest of the window, lighting me up like a spotlight turning on and aimed at my face. I squinted, the view I'd wanted blocked from sight now on full display.

Outside my window, like a stupid fucking painting, was the Royal Palace Rose Garden, currently clinging to life through the frigid colds that had spilled over Madrid during the winter months. And yet *still*, even with the trees bare and the roses out of bloom, the garden somehow retained its imposing beauty. Maybe it was the golden statues scattered throughout, or the two perfectly symmetrical fountainheads on either side of the garden shooting a constant stream of crystalline water feet up into the air. The emerald-green hedges were still holding strong, as were the regal snowdrift crabapple trees we had planted when I was a little boy, their white and red flowers acting like small sun reflectors. Beyond the gardens, I could see the tall crest of the palace itself, a stone spire that rose like a thorn on the side of this earth. It wrapped around the garden, making the roses and crabapple trees a centerpiece of the entire palace.

I royally fucking hated it.

"Look at me, Nicholas. Look at me and tell me you don't want this anymore. Us."

"I'm sorry, but I can't be in this relationship any longer." I said it again, meaning it as much as the first time I'd said it.

"So you're not joking. This isn't some kind of prank."

"I'm not joking. I can't continue this... this..." I said the first word that came to my mouth. "Facade."

She arched her eyebrow as though it were a bow ready to be notched with a lethal arrow.

"A facade? You call what we had a facade?"

"*Sí.*"

I said it matter-of-factly. Not because I felt it was that simple—nothing ever really was that simple. I only said it in the way I did so that the point would be hammered home. She had to hear it. Cristella didn't do well when I beat around the bush. She always had a way of making me second-guess myself, and the more time I allowed her to do that, the more I risked backing down.

And that was the last thing I wanted to do. I felt like I'd already tiptoed off the cliff's edge and was now free-falling through the air.

Exhilarating.

And there was no turning back.

"Okay." Her head started to shake back and forth. A small movement. And then the tears started to flow.

My heart cracked. I knew this would be painful as much as I knew it had to be done, but that didn't ease any of the guilt I felt at seeing her hurt. We had already talked about marriage, kids, a castle, crowns. The entire shebang. She must have been watching that all sink to the bottom of the sea, all her dreams slowly bubbling under the previously serene waters, now raging and tormenting.

"Oh, Crist—"

"Don't do that." She covered her mouth, stifling a cry. Before I could say another word, she turned to the door and bolted. I got off the bed, not bothering to put on anything over my black boxers, and ran after her.

Crossing the threshold of my bedroom was like crossing a portal into a fantasy land. An entirely different world awaited outside of the doorway. Where my bedroom was simple and elegant, the grand hallway I was now running through felt extravagant and overly pompous. The ceiling was arched and elevated, with gold filigree running throughout it, playing with the sunlight that bounced off the always polished white marble floors. There were enormous oil paintings hung up on either side of the hall, blurring past me as I ran, bare feet cold against the smooth floor. Holiday decorations had already been placed, leaving this moment all the more steeped in irony as I chased my crying ex-girl-friend past a row of silver and gold candy canes, directly underneath dangling mistletoes that appeared more like the blades of a guillotine than a Christmas decoration.

"Cristella!"

She turned into a bathroom and slammed the door shut, clicking the heavy lock into place just as I stopped myself from running past it, carried by momentum.

I tried calling her name for a couple more minutes before I heard the click of heels coming from around the corner. I looked down and realized just how close to naked I was. Behind me, an arching window looked out over a small courtyard, devoid of anyone. Still, it wouldn't be long before those heels clicked their way around the corner.

I cursed under my breath and turned on my feet, speed walking down the hallway back toward my bedroom. There was nothing else I could do. I had broken poor Cristella's heart while trying to mend my own. Only time would tell if either of us would ever heal.

"Nicholas?"

I froze, shutting my eyes and wishing I could just vanish in a puff of smoke. Then I turned, facing my mother. She stood next to the window, the sun shining down on her and causing the sapphire necklace she wore to glow as endlessly blue as the sea itself. It popped against her pale skin, high-lighted even more by the black dress she wore, cut just above the ankle and trimmed in silver lace with inlaid pearls.

Meanwhile, I stood there with my ass practically showing.

"Mom."

"Are you... okay?" She started toward me, heels clicking again.

"Yes, yes. All good. I'm going to go shower."

She squinted her eyes. Suspicion had been her middle name ever since I was a child testing the boundaries. She suspected everything I did and always assumed there was a second story lying just underneath the first.

She was right about today, so I'd give her that.

"Aren't you leaving on your trip today?"

"Tomorrow, actually." I started the trek back to my

bedroom, not realizing just how much ground Cristella covered with her run.

"Ah, *bueno*. I'll be asking you to meet with some people while you're overseas. Some light diplomatic things. It won't interfere on your and Cristella's vacation, I promise."

I ground my teeth. Aside from suspicion, my mother was also fond of surprises. She enjoyed springing things on people at the very last second, and I was now feeling the effects of that.

Fine. If she was going to deal a surprise, then so would I.

"Cristella and I broke up."

A tiny gasp sounded from behind me. I stopped at my bedroom door, a snow-dusted wreath hanging on the center of it.

"But... but... *que?*"

For once in her life, it seemed like the queen was at a loss for words.

"It wasn't working out. I'm sorry, Mom. I'm done with living for other people. I'm a prince, not a puppet. I gave it an honest shot and realized I wasn't happy. Done."

She looked dumbfounded. And then the sound of more footsteps coming from the opposite end of the hall drifted toward us. My mother clicked back into queen mode, straightening her shoulders and adopting a neutral expression before looking over my shoulder and offering a smile.

"Ah, *buenos días*, Luna."

If I could breathe a sigh of relief without being obvious, I sure as hell would have.

I turned, smiling and offering a wave.

Luna Rodríguez walked toward us, glancing at me with a mixture of concern and amusement. She was the head of my security team and had watched my back since I could remember ever being worried about it. Behind her bounced Eli, my golden retriever and most trusted confidant. His tongue lolled out as he came over, crashing into my legs, rubbing his big head against my thighs. I pet him, scratching underneath his ears.

"Is everything okay?" my mom asked.

"Sí," Luna answered. "Just came to ask some questions about the trip to America."

"Yeah, about that." I crouched down so that Eli could land some kisses on my cheek. "It's canceled."

"Oh?" Luna looked down in surprise. "So where are you and Cristella going to go?"

"Also canceled."

Her face snapped back up. She looked to my mother, who shot her a look before saying, "I have to go greet the duchess. Please, Luna, talk some sense into this stubborn prince of mine."

She kissed Luna's cheeks and then the top of my head before she whisked down the hall, heels clicking against the floor. I waited until she disappeared before saying, "I need to get out of here, Luna. I really need to go."

"Did something happen?" She had her hands in her black slacks, her expression worried.

"I'm finally doing something for myself," I said, standing back up. Eli sat down at my feet, looking like the happiest dog in the world. "So if you have any suggestions on where I could run away to, I'd love to know."

"Well..." Luna said, thinking as I started to walk down the hall and back to my room. Luna and Eli followed. "Since I'm thinking about your America trip, my parents take a yearly holiday cruise from Miami. They spend something like sixteen days in the Caribbean, and they absolutely love it. When they come back, they look like new people. My mom comes back with a boatload of glamor shots and my dad's bald head comes back with a sunburn."

"Perfect," I said. Being on a cruise ship where I'd know there weren't paparazzi hiding in every bush or tree I walked past sounded like paradise. Add the fact that I doubted I would be recognized by a crowd of vacationing Americans. They had fascinations with royal families that only seemed to extend to England's. Meanwhile, I couldn't walk through most any street in Europe without getting recognized.

A spontaneous breakup and a Caribbean Christmas cruise... I wonder what other surprises this holiday's got in store for me.

2 SHIRO BROOKS

I rolled my suitcase up the smooth concrete ramp, the sun shining into my eyes as I looked up to try and admire the cruise ship. I flicked down my sunglasses, instantly feeling some relief.

The ship towered above us in all its seventeen-deck glory. It was a modern marvel of science and the newest cruise ship to be sailing anywhere in the world. The paint job was a modern work of art, with bold red and blue lines that cut across the side of the ship, underneath the rows and rows of glass windows and balconies that made it almost seem as if the ship were a floating Apple Store.

A line started to form and curl in front of me as people were shuffled through the security checkpoint, leading into a large waiting area since it was still too early to board the ship. I looked around, knowing I wouldn't see any of my friends yet, but still hoping I'd catch a familiar smile.

We haven't all been together in years.

I was excited about this cruise, even if the past few weeks had been one hell of a ride getting here.

No dwelling on the bullshit, though. This trip was about reuniting with old friends during the one season absolutely made for reunions. Which worked especially well since the cruise was advertised as a holiday wonderland. The entire ship was said to have been transformed for the holidays, from a giant stuffed polar bear wearing sunglasses by the pool to a snow pit where you could go and make snow angels after drinking a margarita. There were holiday-themed shows and dance clubs, along with a crazy sweater party and a sexy Santa dance-off. Apparently, there was even a "blizzard" foam party planned.

Needless to say, I had signed up real quick when I saw the ad. Thankfully my friends were all on board for the trip, too. Ever since we scattered across the globe after graduating college, it had been hard to all be in the same spot, but these next three weeks were about to fix all that.

I inched forward in line. My shoulders, tense all this past week, were finally relaxed. I took in a deep breath of the ocean air. Miami never got cold, but today was a little on the chillier side. At seventy-one, native Miamians were pulling out their scarves and mittens.

A commotion from behind me drew my attention. I leaned out of the line and glanced at the source of two loud, overly excited voices.

"That's him, that's him, that's totally him," one of the girls was saying, almost shouting. She had a death grip on her friend's elbow, which I could see was beginning to lose color.

"Is it?" the one in danger of losing her arm asked.

One of the boys they were with just shouts, "Are you that Avenger guy?".

The girl with the loose ponytail shook her head, her cheeks turning a bright cherry red. "Not from Avengers. The brother. Liam. You're Liam Hemsworth?"

I looked to see who they were talking to and spot someone who had to have been a celebrity, and if they weren't, then they were working in the wrong field.

The man wore a simple, all-black outfit, with clean white sneakers and a watch with a worn leather band. He had a black hat on his head, the lip of it brought down so that the top half of his face was concealed in shadow.

The lower half, though. *Duh-damn*. That was more than enough for me. He had a little bit of well-taken-care-of scruff, trimmed to the skin at his Adam's apple and down. His lips were drawn into an entertained smirk, slanting in the same way his jawline did.

"No," I heard him say. "I'm no one."

The dad of the two girls picked up on the situation. He apologized and brought the girls back to their spot in line, which they had apparently jumped to try and get a better look at the mystery "no one." I didn't blame them either.

"Excuse me, sir, the line's moving."

"Oh shoot, sorry," I said, turning and realizing I had been standing still while a good four-foot gap formed in the line as people shuffled forward. I made sure not to slip on the drool that had pooled at my feet.

Clearly, I was a little boy-crazy, which I shouldn't be

considering that the guy I'd been dating for the past year broke up with me because he saw a documentary on a religion dedicated to the Rolling Stones and decided to go join it. When I said "abso-fucking-lutely not" to joining when he asked, he said he understood but that we wouldn't be able to stay together. I had thought it was an elaborate prank for a good half hour, until I realized he was being fully serious.

"Can you even name one Rolling Stones song?" I remembered asking him.

He rattled off a couple titles, none of them sounding familiar to me, which wasn't a surprise seeing as how I for sure wouldn't be able to name a single Rolling Stones song.

The security checkpoint cleared up ahead. I went through, letting them check my suitcase and scan me with those metal wands. The security officer—Lionel, read the tag, with a tiny mistletoe over his name—asked me to turn around. I faced the rest of the line, my gaze instantly finding that mysterious man with the sexy jaw and the cap, which was now flipped so that I could see the rest of his face.

Holy crapola, this man was everything. I wasn't sure what I liked better, the top half of his face or the previously introduced bottom half?

Then again, why not have both?

His eyes—wow, they were multidimensional, like two little blue-and-gray galaxies held inside the most perfectly sculpted face. He had a strong brow and thick eyebrows that added a frame to a picture I could stare at all day and night.

Especially night.

Lionel waved the wand over my shoulder and down my

back before he ran it over the front of my chest and then down over my shorts.

A loud beeping sounded. Directly above my penis.

"Oh, that's, um, weird."

Lionel tried again. More beeping as he held the wand right on top of my crotch. I could see people in line beginning to look in my direction, but thankfully, the handsome man straight out of my dreams (and most likely my league) had his attention held by something on his phone. I guessed that I had approximately fifteen seconds before he looked up and saw me getting dragged away for a weaponized penis.

"It's nothing," I said, turning to Lionel. "The zipper maybe?"

"Do you have any piercings?"

"Oh no, just the thought of that is making me contract into my own body." I pursed my lips. "Which is probably too much information."

"We have an area to the left where another agent can check you." Lionel motioned to what appeared to be a makeshift changeroom, ignoring my mention of an inverting dick. It was a circular area concealed by a wrinkled blue sheet. I wanted to roll my eyes and assure Lionel I had nothing between my legs that needed to be checked, at least not by security. But, on the same token, he was just doing his job and making sure every passenger stayed safe. I turned and walked to another security officer, who led me into the changing room.

"I think my zipper triggered it."

The officer, a muscular guy with an impressive forearm tattoo of a roaring lion, offered me a surprisingly apologetic smile. "The sensor's been a little sensitive. I'm just going to ask you to take your shorts and shirt off for a quick search, and then you can board."

I glanced around at the flimsy blue curtain. If I looked hard enough, I could make out faces through small holes that dotted the fabric. I felt my cheeks turn a fiery red. Not because I had to have a surprise strip search, but because that handsome god of a man was standing feet away from me as I began to undress. It was an odd place for my brain to go, but I couldn't help it as I started to wonder if he could see me, if he could see the shape of me through the shadows on the curtain. I took off my shirt and went for my shorts next, not remembering what underwear I had put on but knowing that it at least wasn't one of my jockstraps.

I unzipped my shorts and took them off. My briefs were bright yellow with cartoon bananas playfully placed around them, the band around my hips was jet black. I faced the officer and tried not to think about the fact that my briefs looked a little more full than they normally did.

Handsome Cap Man is doing things to me without even being near me.

The officer used the wand again, quickly swiping it up and down, the machine staying quiet this time. He then personally checked my shorts, flipping the pockets inside out. When he was done, he handed back my shorts and turned around so I could change.

"Is that it?" I asked.

"Yup, that's it. Thanks for cooperating."

I nodded and "mhmmed" as I lifted a leg to put my shorts back on.

That's when things went from "fine" to "what in the actual fuck is my life" all in about fifteen seconds flat.

As I was lifting my leg, I lost my balance. Normally, I'm not a clumsy guy. I competed in gymnastics all throughout high school and college, even making it up to the Olympic qualifiers before I took a terrible fall off the pommel horse and had to take two years off to recover. Since then, I never got back into gymnastics, instead finding a new passion in parkour, joining a team who'd practice inside of one of their home gyms before we went out to the streets.

This meant that I could stick a landing, but only when that landing wasn't concealed by a flimsy blue curtain. I snatched for it, hearing a loud tear as the fabric fell with me. I rolled up in the thing like a blue burrito, cushioning my fall and potentially sparing me from a broken rib or two.

"Whoa!" The security officer who had searched me somehow managed to get wrapped up in my mess. I looked up, feeling my cheeks heat as I tried to swim out of the tangled-up cloth, only realizing once I was free that I was also near naked. I stood there, the entire line watching me with dropped jaws, wearing only my goddamn banana briefs. Nothing simple and elegant and worthy of an impromptu underwear modeling session. Instead, it was a bold and graphic print that drew everyone's attention.

I locked eyes with the handsome stranger and almost self-combusted. I wasn't exactly shy of my body and didn't mind showing it off now and then, but the stranger's gaze did something to me. Turned me into a meek little kid, standing there exposed, as if on stage and under a spotlight. Literally a worst-nightmare kind of situation.

And then the stranger smiled. His lips tilted into a

smirk, his eyes still covered by the hat. It was a smile that pushed away my shame. Replaced it with something else, something fiery and sudden and potent. A smile that made the entire rest of the gawking crowd disappear, as if they were all part of an elaborate magic trick.

The meek child disappeared, too, taken over by a powerful need that stemmed deep in my gut.

"Here, let's, uh, head to the bathroom." The officer, whose cheeks were as red as mine felt, walked over to me and handed me my shorts, which I quickly tugged on before grabbing my shirt and socks and heading to the bathroom, my head held high even though my back felt like flames were licking up my spine. I could almost pinpoint where on my body the stranger's eyes had landed, and where they were pinned to now.

In the bathroom, I finished getting dressed. The fluorescent light lit up my face as I looked in the mirror, shaking my head with a smile, wondering what the hell this Christmas cruise had in store for me.

3   NICHOLAS SILVA

Over the many years of growing up and having an assortment of eyes trained on you at all times, I had developed a keen sense of knowing when someone was looking at me. Sometimes it came in handy and helped me avoid unwanted snaps of me from leaking; other times it kept me feeling like a paranoid mess that couldn't just relax in the moment. I understood that I stuck out from the crowd, regardless of what country I was in. I stood at a tall six foot four inches, and I had a presence that could turn heads whenever I walked into a room, so it wasn't like having eyes on me was a rare occasion.

As I stood in line waiting to board the cruise ship, I had felt many different eyes graze over me. I scoped out the crowd and didn't find many that I'd want to chat with, except for the one guy who had been quite bold in his staring. I noticed it when the girls called me out for thinking I was a celebrity, which did get me slightly nervous, but I knew that judging by their age alone they most likely had no idea who Spain's prime minister was, much less who was in their royal family.

I let my thoughts drift, focusing in on the handsome man and his bold stare, wondering if this cruise would be the perfect opportunity to stretch my closeted wings and experience what I'd been wanting to for years now.

The way my dick twitched at the thought only confirmed it for me.

A muffled shout drew my attention. The half-naked and perfect-bodied man held it.

It was him. The man who had been throwing looks at me. He stood there after breaking free from his blue prison, looking stunned in the same way I felt.

Except, unlike him, I was stunned because of how fucking perfect this man was. He was no longer concealed by the line of people ahead of me (or his clothes, for that matter), and the way he stood really didn't leave much to the imagination, especially since his briefs were extremely well fitting.

I'd never been with another guy before, but that didn't stop me from drooling over this one. He was everything I would jerk off to in secret, the guys I'd click on and watch as they played with themselves and one another. He had a chest I wanted to grab and bite, and a tight stomach that showed a six-pack I wanted to run my hands over, with a hint of a treasure trail that looked perfect for tracing with my tongue.

And those obliques. Holy motherfucking shit. The Vmuscles that pointed down at those banana briefs like they were advertising a hot sale were sculpted out of fucking marble.

Coño. This guy is everything.

Then our eyes met, and the guy who looked like everything suddenly *felt* like everything, too. It was difficult to explain, and even more difficult to believe. But in just that one fleeting glance, I felt like an entire world of questions had been answered for me. Like I was staring at the key holder to a long-locked part of me.

And then he disappeared, pulling on his shorts and hurrying to the bathroom, leaving me behind, shell-shocked at what had just happened. I hadn't realized the line had started to move again until someone tapped me on my shoulder and pointed.

"Are you okay?"

The finger belonged to Luna. She wore a wide-brimmed tourist hat and tortoise-patterned sunglasses that seemed one size too big for her face. She normally kept a farther distance from me when I requested it, but the loud situation involving my dream man must have drawn her over. I couldn't see her eyes, but I could tell just by her body position that she was ready to react. She had a hand underneath her oversized button-up teal shirt dotted with multicolored flowers, no doubt over her concealed pistol.

"I'm fine, I'm fine."

She looked around me, at the officers who were fixing up the private screening area. "*Bueno.*" She nodded and took her hand out from her shirt. "I'm not a fan of being the only one on security detail here, just for the record, Nick."

"I know. Thank you, Luna. I appreciate it." And I did. It

had taken a shit ton of convincing to allow this trip to happen, and a lot of precautions taken before hand. "I just wanted to keep this trip as quiet as possible. I've been dealing with enough back home. I really didn't want to bring an entire troop of guards and have everyone wonder who the hell I was."

"Just don't go doing anything crazy. Always keep me in mind. I know you can get carried away sometimes."

"Me? Ridiculous," I said as I was actively being carried away on thoughts of where that sexy banana boy had gone.

Luna went back to her spot in line as I moved up, reaching the security checkpoint. I walked through and into the waiting area before boarding the ship. It felt like a large, modern warehouse, with glass ceilings that showered the space in bright light. There were food stands and supply shops against the wall, along with an abundance of sleek white tables and chairs. A thick palm tree grew in the center of the room, surrounded by benches, a few trickling water fountains set throughout.

I wasn't paying attention to any of it. Sure, it registered in the back of my head, but my focus was on finding banana boy, even if it was just for me to steal an extra glance. We were going to be on the same ship for the next twenty-one days, so I figured we would *have* to bump into each other at some point.

I looked around, walking through the thick crowd, growing as more people filed in through security. Kids were happily running around, some playing tag, others finding spots to sit where they could play games with their friends, cousins, siblings. The energy was high as the space filled with the constant din of excited conversations. People were taking selfies galore, and thankfully, none of them were asking to take one with me.

Just ahead of me was a bookstore: Port Pages. Above the wood-framed door was a neon blue, red, and white sign depicting a toy boat jumping into an open book, the name of the bookstore flashing above it. I shrugged, thinking if I couldn't find that sexy banana-briefed guy, then I could at least find a good book to get lost in. Reading a page-turning mystery while working on my holiday tan sounded like a fun way to spend an afternoon or three.

Inside, the bookstore felt much cozier than the grand and airy waiting area. Instead of glass and steel, wooden shelves and tucked-away nooks dominated the aesthetic. I almost didn't even recognize the checkout counter, which was between two tall stacks of thick, leather-bound books. It smelled just like the library back in the palace, a place I'd enjoy getting lost in for hours on end, especially as a kid, when my attention span didn't feel like it was as brittle as a burnt tree, ready to snap if I strained it for longer than five minutes.

I walked through the aisles, my suitcase rolling along beside me. I let go of the handle and reached for a book that caught my interest, its cover depicting a silky blue backdrop with an elaborate dagger tucked in the center.

That's when I spotted him. Banana boy. He was idly walking through the center aisle, his head slowly nodding as he read the different spines, most likely trying to decide which one he'd pick up. For some reason, I had an urge to peek into his thoughts, figure out what he liked to read, what he wanted to spend hours curled up with. Did he enjoy hard-boiled mysteries, or was he more of a romantic-comedy kind of guy? Did he like reading fantasy adventures or sci-fi rides through the final frontier? He turned into a section that blocked him from view.

I followed. It felt like some kind of primal pull, like there had been an invisible rope tied to the both of our waists.

The aisle he walked into was a dead end. He focused on a book with a hot-pink spine. He reached for it when I said, "Hey there, banana boy."

He turned on his heels, eyes opened wide in surprise. "Oh, uh, hey, hi."

It appeared as if I lit a match underneath his cheeks with how red they turned. "Nice show you gave earlier."

"You're lucky," he said, finding his footing. "Usually it's way more expensive."

"Oh?"

He nodded before chuckling, a nervous sound that I wanted to drink up. We stood between two tall bookshelves that reached up to the ceiling. One wall held more books, their colorful covers facing us, adding a backdrop of rainbow to the man who smiled in technicolor.

"Just joking. I've never charged before," he said before he added, "I guess there's always a first time for everything, though."

I laughed, the sound in the quiet space surprising me. "There certainly is." I offered a smile to match banana boy's as I reached up and flipped my hat, moving the shadows from my face. Tucked away in the back of this bookstore, I felt safe. I knew no one would be taking secret photos or throwing prolonged glances.

It didn't seem like banana boy recognized me either,

although he did seem a little taken aback when I flipped my hat. I saw a brief crack in his expression before he composed himself.

"This is my first time on a cruise," I offered, wanting to keep the conversation going between us two.

"Really? You're gonna love it. Soft-serve ice cream at any time of the day really makes any experience worthwhile."

"I'm looking forward to it."

And to bumping into you.

"I'm Shiro Brooks, by the way. You can call me Shy."

"Nice to meet you, Shy." His smirk said he was a lot of things but shy. We shook hands, an action that felt much too formal for a man who I already envisioned naked with his legs wrapped tight around me.

I had to do a quick calculation just then. Did I offer him my real name, potentially handing him a key to figuring out who I really was? Or did I go the alias route, covering as much of my tracks as I could?

It was a choice that, if wrong, could really fuck up my time on the ship. A time meant for me to figure myself out and find a kind of peace and happiness I'd been missing in my life for a very long time. It should have been easy to lie to this virtual stranger, and yet, for some reason, his bright brown eyes convinced me that he was the most trustworthy human being on this entire planet.

"Nick," I said, making a decision I could very much come to regret later. I reasoned with myself that I still didn't give him my full name, but it didn't take much of a leap to go from Nick to Nicholas.

"Nice to meet you, Nick."

Our hands were still shaking. Barely shaking, but still connected. Through our palms ran an undeniable current. The hair on the back of my arm rose. I didn't want to let go. I wanted to grab his hand and pull him to me. I wondered how he would feel against me, how different he would be compared to Cristella.

"Do you, um, like to..." Shiro looked around us. "Read?"

Our hands separated on a laugh. "I do, sí."

"Are you from Miami?" Shiro must have picked up on my accent. Another clue I inadvertently dropped for him.

"No, I'm not." More calculations in my head. I was always a bit of a risk-taker, and so the numbers landed on the "why not" side. "I'm from Spain."

"Ohhh, a Spaniard." Shiro looked me up and down. I did the same with him, taking a moment to actually admire him. The way he stood, with his legs slightly apart and his hands at ease by his sides. How he looked in his pressed khaki shorts, cut an inch above the knee, and how his thighs pressed against the hem. His shirt hugged him tight, too, showing off some of the curvature from the muscles underneath. He was a little shorter than me but still taller than average, with a build that made it clear he stayed fit.

"And where are you from?" I asked, trying hard not to stare openly at his lips.

"Born in Osaka, Japan, before my mom moved to be with my father. He's American—they met when he was teaching English over there. We moved to Miami when I was around two."

"I love the time I've spent in Japan. Haven't gotten to go to Osaka but I had a blast in Tokyo and Kyoto."

"Ohh, Kyoto is beautiful, isn't it? The Buddhist temples are something else."

"They sure are," I said. "Do you go back to Osaka often?"

"We try to go back once every two years or so." He cocked his head, smiling at me in a way I couldn't quite read. His eyes bounced from mine to my lips. "And you?" he asked, "What brought you all the way from Spain? Is this holiday cruise really that popular?"

I laughed, toying with the cap on my head. No one had walked past our little nook, making this moment feel all the more private. There weren't even any voices around us. I wondered if people were already beginning to board.

"I heard there would be five-star entertainment on the ship. Something about an extremely attractive man in tiny and slightly see-through banana underwear."

"Okay, they weren't tiny." Shiro cocked his head, his lips pursed into a tight smile. "*That* tiny. And maybe they were slightly see-through."

"Let's just say, I could tell your banana doesn't have the peel on it."

Shiro's eyes opened wide, his cheeks turning rose-petal red.

"Joking," I said, wondering if I'd gone too far. What had pushed me to go that far? We'd only just met and I was already making dick jokes...

"Well, your joke isn't exactly far from the truth." Although Shiro's cheeks still blushed, his stance and his gaze radiated confidence. He crossed his arms, his chest muscles perking up, his biceps looking larger, too. He licked his lips. I wondered if it was subconscious or calculated. If he knew how crazy he was beginning to drive me. "Did you enjoy the preboarding show? Are you leaving me five Yelp stars?"

"I was considering it, but I felt like it ended too soon. May drop it down to four."

"Oh yeah?"

"I could have watched for hours. I only got barely a minute."

"Well..." Shiro moved closer to me. My heartbeat began to thrum louder and faster. I wondered if he could hear it in the encapsulating silence of the bookstore. "Maybe I can do something to bump up that review. Five stars."

"For?"

"For this."

He had read me, as if he had picked me up from one of the surrounding shelves and flipped through my pages. He knew I wanted him, as badly as he seemed to want me. No more wasting time. I couldn't explain it if I tried, but on the same token, I felt like I didn't have to. My entire life had been centered around me explaining myself. Having to answer to everyone else's expectations, never considering my own. Never taking into account what I really wanted, for fear I'd upset everyone else around me. That ended with my empty relationship. I was done with wasting time. That's what this trip was about: living my life the way I wanted to. I made that choice on the morning I had walked home from Hightower Bridge.

And right now, I wanted to make out with the sexiest man I'd ever laid eyes on in the seclusion of an empty bookstore.

His lips grazed mine, tentative at first, his hand coming

up to my head, mine to the back of his neck. Our heads moved to a silent beat, finding the rhythm we could both dance to. He tasted like a candy cane, minty and fresh. I wanted more of it. More of him.

My tongue licked at his lips, fanning the flames that consumed me from my toes to my scalp. He parted for me, allowing me in, giving me more of his taste, more of him. I took it, probing him with my tongue, his other hand moving from my hip to my ass. I felt a shock run through me as he squeezed, pushing me onto him. A moan rose from me, uncontrolled, one he greedily swallowed.

The kiss exploded, faster and more passionate than anything I'd felt before. It hit out of nowhere, like a bolt of pure lightning striking from a cloudless and sapphire-blue sky.

But before we could get carried away and start a fire with all this kindle around us, I knew that I had to stop. This had been beyond risky. This bordered on insane. Sure, I could live life on the edge, but this was us plummeting *off* the edge. If anyone got a photo of this, I would... fuck. I don't even know what would happen.

When we broke apart, our lips still shiny from the kiss, I looked past Shiro, hoping against all hope that there wasn't someone at the end of the aisle with their camera phone aimed at us, reeling in a story that was bound to sell for thousands.

There was no one with a camera, thankfully. In that moment ,though, someone did cross the aisle, staring directly at me for a brief second before flitting away.

Luna. She had kept her distance from me like I asked,

but of course she didn't like having her eyes off me for very long.

Damn it. Did she see the kiss, too?

"You okay?" Shiro asked me, glancing over his shoulder.

"Yeah, why?"

"You look like you were looking for something. I was scared it was for an escape route."

I laughed at that, sucking on my lower lip, as if that would give me the taste my body now craved. "Definitely not," I assured him.

"Okay, good. Because running was the last thing on my mind after that kiss."

"What was the first thing?"

Shiro's lips quirked. "When round two would be."

That cocky, banana-brief-wearing fucker. Already assuming round two was a sure thing.

"Now," I answered him, pulling him by his hips into my body, my lips finding his again, only then being filled with the taste I was beginning to crave. Starting to *need*. His tongue pressed against my lips, parting them open, him feeling just as needy as me. I could feel his hard body push against mine. I took a step backward, stumbling, my back hitting the shelves. Nothing fell, so we continued, an endless reservoir of untapped passion fueling this out-of-control wildfire.

And then I remembered we were in public. As hard as it was (and trust me, it was fucking *hard*), I separated from Shiro's lips, the both of us breathless. We looked into each other's eyes then and shared something unspoken but powerful all the same.

This had been a collision course set in motion from the

moment I spotted him standing at the security line. We had crossed time spans in the blink of an eye, in the taste of a kiss.

Shiro was no longer a stranger, even though that's all he was five minutes ago.

"Wow," he said. He ran a thumb across his lip, some of the gloss from our kiss wiping off.

He looked up at me, inquisitive eyes pinning me in place. I could almost see the gears turning behind them. It appeared as if he'd been hit with some kind of idea, the way his eyes narrowed and how he chewed on the inside of his lip.

It was my turn to ask, "Are *you* okay?"

"Better than okay," he said, laughing, gears still spinning. "All right, so this is a really nuts idea. Like, batshit, off-the-wall kind of crazy, but follow along with me."

I knit my brows together. "Are you about to rob me or something?"

"No, no. I'm about to potentially make a huge fool of myself is what I'm about to do. But it could... I don't know, it could make this Christmas one for the books." Shiro motioned around us. "Get it?"

"Mhmm," I said, laughing. "I do."

"Ok, because if you didn't then I'd be worried."

"I would be too." More laughing. There was a pink blush that seemed to spread from his cheeks. He had me intrigued. I couldn't imagine him doing anything that would make me think him a fool. Shiro squeezed his hands together as if he were drying a rag above a sink. "But, I don't know, that kiss, it... shit, I think it got me drunk or something. So, okay, this cruise, it's a kind of reunion for me and my friends. We booked it months ago, and we haven't seen each other in years, so it's kind of a big moment..."

The nervous smile on his face grew. He looked almost bashful to me, his butterfly lashes flicking up and down. I wasn't sure where this was going, but I didn't mind following Shiro to wherever he led me.

4 SHIRO BROOKS

One for the books? Jesus, I couldn't think of anything better?

And still, I was allowing the word vomit to continue: "We're all meeting up for this cruise and... well, everyone's paired up. I'm the only one showing up single."

Seriously. Pump the brakes on this out-of-control sleigh ride.

"And so..."

This was my chance. I could just say forget it, thank you for the kiss, and I hope to bump into you again sometime.

Instead, I spit out: "So you should be my fake boyfriend. For the cruise. Just, you know, for fun."

Nick's face went blank. As if he had trouble hearing what I was proposing, even though you could hear a damn pin drop and do the cha-cha across the floor with how quiet this bookstore was.

"I saw this movie last night," I barreled on, feeling as if I had to explain myself, "and it gave me the idea. We don't have to do any of the real boyfriend stuff. We'll set rules. No sex and you know, other stuff..."

Nick cocked his head to the side. "What kind of other stuff?"

"Oh, so that part you want to ask about?"

His smile flashed before it went out like a broken Christmas light. "A fake boyfriend?" he asked again, as if he couldn't hear me over the roaring sound of closed books.

"Yes..." Should I be backtracking? Nick's smile, his kiss, his eyes, they all fried my brain, turning my thoughts into scrambled eggs. Maybe I'd had a temporary moment of dick-sanity. Maybe I should be telling him it was all a mistake...

But what if he agreed to my crazy plan?

He bit his bottom lip, his eyes casting down at the floor. This wasn't the expression of a man who was about to agree to be my fake boyfriend for a few weeks.

My phone buzzed in my pocket. I glanced at my Apple Watch and quickly read the text message from Jada: *We're all on the ship, in the atrium! Where r u?*

I'm currently making a damn fool of myself, is where I am.

Nick looked back up from the floor, his blue-gold eyes reflecting enough light that he could easily cosplay as a lighthouse. A sexy lighthouse.

Now that would be a good Halloween costume.

"Shy, being your fake boyfriend actually sounds like exactly what I need on this trip."

So then why was I sensing a "but" just around the corner—and not the good kind of butts, the ones I liked to squeeze.

"*Pero...*"

Ah, the Spanish "but," one of my favorite kinds. I opened my mouth to tell him forget about it. Nick cut me off.

"I can't. I'm sorry."

I knew it was coming, and yet still, it felt like a fresh slap from a jellyfish. In the span of fifteen seconds, I had made myself over-the-moon excited at the idea of even being fake boyfriends with this handsome Prince Charming. It felt like the perfect way to stick it to Mason, while having fun on my vacation and avoiding any awkward convos at the same time.

"Right, I get it," I said, having a hard time getting it. We clearly had chemistry, and sure I didn't even know his last name, but wasn't that all part of the fun? The discovery of it all?

His beautiful (ugh, I mean annoying) lips turned down into a frown. "I don't mean it as in I wouldn't *like* being your boyfriend. Fake or otherwise. It's just... complicated. Very fucking complicated."

I nodded, trying to keep it as chill as I could. "It was a dumb idea," I said, throwing dirt on the dying fire between us.

"No, it wasn't dumb at all."

I wanted to ask him why couldn't he just say yes then, but the last thing I wanted to do was push on an already dead idea. Whatever, I'd just go meet up with my friends and have a good time on this cruise, even if I did end up being the seventh wheel.

A sound from the aisle over made us both perk up. For some reason, being with Nick in this private corner made it feel as if we had taken a rocket ship up into orbit, where no one else could bother us, where no one could see me making a complete fool of myself.

I pointed a thumb over my shoulder. "All right, well, we should get going. I think they're boarding the ship."

"Right, we should..."

"What?"

He licked his lips. I knew what was coming next, and I didn't fight it in the slightest. Nick reached up, both hands on either side of my face, and he kissed me. It must have been meant as a "goodbye" kiss, a "one last time" kiss.

So why did it feel like a "just beginning" kiss?

I walked out of the bookshop wiping at my lips. I didn't want to be smiling, considering how I had just had my hopes dashed, and yet my lips wouldn't stop curling. I still felt like a flustered mess, though, as I made my way through the big warehouse waiting area and onto the ship. The entire way there, I kept mentally reprimanding myself, reliving the moment I had lost all sense and blurted out a question that would surely haunt me for the rest of my life. Like the ghost of embarrassing Christmas past, coming at me in the middle of the night, rattling chains and whispering the words "boyfriend, fake, please" over and over again.

I shook off a chill but couldn't shake off the feeling of regret that followed me as I swam my way through the growing crowd, going up the ramp and stepping onto the ship for the first time, being greeted by a smiling worker who let me know where my cabin would be. I walked straight ahead, the corridor having been transformed into a holiday wonderland, with fake snow crunching under my feet, the red floor underneath popping through the track marks left behind by the rolling suitcases. There was a wooden signpost at the end of the hall, pointing the way to the food court, the atrium, the pool, and the North Pole.

I went left, toward the atrium, through a curving gold-and-white-striped walkway. There were large sticks of cinnamon resting in tall, clear vases, filling the air with their scent, making it feel like I was walking through a busy bakery, their display cases filled with warm holiday treats.

The ship's atrium could only be described as grand, made even more so by the elegant touch of Christmas decorations set throughout. The atrium was all about subtlety. There were wreaths made of tinsel and red ribbon-covered garland hanging on the gold-trimmed oak walls. A scattering of hand-sized snowflakes had been dusted on the glass walls of the elevator, and the curving staircase had its banister wrapped in garland. The centerpiece of the room was the twelve-foot-tall pine tree, the branches full and thick with pine needles, a string of white lights placed perfectly in spiraling rows up its entire length. There were ornaments glittering against the white lights, gold and silver and royal blue. A mixture of balls and stars and icicles. At the very top, the tree was crowned with a large star radiating light, bright enough to shine even through the sunlight that streamed in through the glass ceiling.

I looked around the crowd, feeling my near-deadly case

of embarrassment and self-inflicted dumbassery begin to wane. The shame was being replaced by a buzzing excitement that started off low and blasted right to the sky the second I spotted my friends.

Jada and I made eye contact first. Her squeal alerted the rest, the two of them whipping around and breaking out into wide smiles.

I ran over to them, my heart already feeling full to the brim.

"You guys!" I shouted as the group all came in for hugs, shouts and squeals of excitement filling the air. It felt so good hugging my friends again, after having been apart for years. Like I had just walked into my mom's kitchen after having spent months away at college, smelling her cooking for the first time, the spices and warmth reminding me of easier times.

I put my hands on Lou's shoulders, shaking him, surprised at how big he looked. He used to be as frail as a twig and now looked just as muscular as me. Jada had an arm looped around my waist, her head on my shoulder, her soft brown curls smelling like coconut, just like they had on the days we'd all run off to the beach and lie out, gossiping and laughing and listening to music for the entire day.

Ace clapped his hands and bounced up and down on his heels next to me, his smile lighting up his youthful face. If the three of us had all changed in some way or another, Ace had remained the same, his face somehow being preserved as if he'd just popped out of a time capsule after being frozen in time. He still had his one dimple and his almost perfectly placed beauty marks dotting his unwrinkled face.

Damn him. Damn him to youthful hell.

"This is insane, you guys," Ace said, looking around at the group. "How long has it been since we've all been together?"

"Like four years now. Since we graduated college and got scattered in the postgrad wind," Jada said, her hair brushing my ear as she separated from me.

I cleared my throat. "Well, we've got to promise never to go that long again." Being around my crew felt good. I realized I had gone a good three minutes without thinking about Nick and my crazy-ass proposal. My cheeks flushed with warmth.

Well, three minutes is a record at least.

"We've got to introduce the significant others," Ace cheerily said and turned to the smiling man behind him. He was taller than Ace by a good foot, by my guess, and he seemed older, too, with smile lines that crinkled the space next to his big green eyes, which popped against the pastel-yellow shirt he was wearing. "This is Rex."

Because of course the most innocent appearing one of us would go out and find a man named Rex who looked like he could split him in half with a look alone.

I had to remember to have a secret toast with Ace—he'd done well.

"And this is Ken." It was Jada's turn, who reached for Ken's hand, their fingers locking in what appeared to be a vise grip. I could almost see Ken's dark skin go pale at the force.

"He's an EMT. We met on the field."

"Not over something gruesome, I hope?" Lou asked, his

girlfriend standing next to him but lost in something on her phone.

"Oh no," Ken said, waving a hand in the air. "It was one of the most benign calls I'd ever gotten actually. We thought it was an actual emergency at first, but we get to the house and it's Edith Windham asking for us to open her jar of Nutella. So I credit Nutella for a lot of my happiness," Ken said, laughing.

"So do I," Jada echoed.

"Can I credit Nutella for my happiness, too?" I chimed in.

Ken definitely complemented Jada, standing only a little taller than her and having similar curly brown hair, except his curls were much tighter than Jada's. He had a genuine smile that made me trust him right away. I felt like I had a good sense of character, especially after working the past year at Stonewall Investigations, and Ken struck me as a good guy.

"Speaking of your happiness," Ace said, crossing his hands, "where's Mason?"

"Eh, right. Mason."

Shit... crap.

I should have just been honest with them from the start. I should have texted the group chat and said Mason and I were done. It was made especially difficult because we all knew Mason. He wasn't someone I'd just be introducing to the group. Mason had gone to school with us and had always been around in some capacity or another. It just so happened that a couple of years ago, we each had a bottle of wine and ended up divulging a lot of mutually shared and mutually repressed feelings for the other. We started dating and had a decent go of it.

And now, here I was, standing as the lone ranger, having to stumble my way into a "we broke up" speech and potentially dampen the holiday reunion.

A finger tapped me on my shoulder. I silently said a "thank god" and turned, quickly following it up with a silent "what the fuck?"

Nick stood there, a friendly smile on his handsome, unobscured face, his cap flipped so that a tuft of jet-black hair fell out, catching the sunlight that fell from the glass ceiling in waves. He held out something in his hand, and it took me a moment to realize he meant for me to grab it.

"Here, you dropped this back there, Shy."

I grabbed the ChapStick, placing it in the pocket where my ChapStick already was. "Thank you," I said, confused as all hell.

"These your friends?"

"Um, yeah," I said, thinking quick. "Everyone, this is Ni—"

"Neal. And I'm Shy's bo—"

"He's my friend," I jumped back in. "Mainly Mason's friend. He couldn't make it, so Mason sent *Neal* in his place. Didn't want to waste his ticket."

This had ratcheted up to a new level of odd. Why was Nick changing his mind, and name, for that matter? I was fine playing this game, but I had to clarify the friend part, because I wasn't about to jump back into the fake-boyfriend thing when I wasn't even sure of this guy's real name. Fake friends would be fine for now.

"All right," I said, looking around at the group, a Mariah

Carey holiday classic playing over the speakers. "Let's drop off our things and explore the ship. Everyone meet on the dick in—"

"Did you... just say dick?" Ace asked in a singsong voice, eyes wider than normal.

"No, I didn't."

"Yes, you did," Nick-Neal said in a cocky tone, with a smirk I wanted to kiss right off his face.

"I think I'd know if I said dick instead of deck... damn it. I said dick, didn't I?"

The group started to laugh. Even with the addition of a complete (and devastatingly handsome) stranger, for some reason, maybe because it was the Christmas season, I felt like I was suddenly surrounded by immediate family. A warmth filled my heart, tingling its way through me. I still wondered why the hell I had two ChapSticks in my pocket and a new fake friend who had just shared a mind-blowing and secret kiss with me, a kiss I would replay in every one of my fantasies for the foreseeable and discernable future.

Well, this is *supposed to be the most wonderful time of year...*

5 NICHOLAS SILVA

I had left my suitcase in my suite and freshened up before heading to the deck. Or dick, as Shy liked to refer to it as.

I found myself excited to see him, even though we'd just separated something like fifteen minutes ago. He was entertaining in all kinds of ways. Not just in the fact that he was more than easy to look at, but he was also quick-witted and fun to talk with. I could tell he'd be fun to toy with, too.

But we're just friends. Fake friends, for that matter.

Which, honestly, would probably serve us both better. When I went up to him, I had been thinking with everything but my head. I followed what my heart shouted for— and my dick twitched for. I wanted Shiro—that kiss had left me with a craving I had to feed. So I spotted him in the crowd and approached him, ready to play the part of his fake boyfriend. If some kind of news leaked off the ship, then I'd deal with it then. For now, I was going to chase the object of my intense desire.

We stood on the deck as it started to fill with more passengers, hanging out until the ship's departure. The sun was high up in the sky, a curvy white cloud inching its way over, shading the cruise ship inch by inch. The pool, still closed, was in front of us, and a large polar bear sculpture stood on its two hind legs and appeared to be dipping its clawed toe into the pool. Shiro leaned an elbow on the standing tabletop we stood next to, resting his head on his fist as he looked out at Miami Bay.

"You lied to them," I said, wanting to talk before his friends joined us.

"Yes, I know that." He tilted his head, not moving it off his fist. The way the sunlight played with the yellow and gold in his eyes cast a spell on me. "Are you also responsible for steering this ship, Captain Obvious?"

I arched a brow. Shiro had a spiciness to him. I liked it— I enjoyed batting a little with some back-and-forth.

"If you're a pathological liar, I'd like to know now before we really do go on with this fake friendship."

"Pathological liar? Then why'd you tell everyone your name was Neal when you told me it was Nick?"

That lie had taken even me by surprise. I wasn't set on lying to them, but the way one of them was looking at me— Ace I think his name was—I felt like he may have known something. Of course, I couldn't tell any of this to Shiro, so I just had to dodge around it.

"I use my middle name more often than my first."

"So what do I call you?" I could tell Shiro was trying to

figure out whether he could trust me or not. His eyes bounced between mine. His tongue pushed at his upper lip.

"You can call me Nick."

His face scrunched. "Fine, Nick. Here's the thing. I don't need your fake friendship. I just wanted to dodge the boyfriend question, and you came up at a convenient time. You're technically my douchebag ex's friend, so you can go do whatever you want. Spend your holidays judging someone else."

That shocked me. "I'm not judging anyone." Did he really think that's what I was doing? The one who'd been scared of judgment his entire life. I knew the pain of having a magnifying lens tuned to every part of your existence, and I would never want to turn that magnifying glass against someone else.

"I'm not judging you," I said, a little more forcefully.

He looked up at me with a pair of amber-brown eyes that almost knocked me right off the banister and into the water.

"Well, either way." He brought his reflective sunglasses down on his face, leaving me with a view of myself and hiding those liquid-gold orbs. "You don't have to be my fake friend."

"All right, fine. Forget about the fake part." I leaned back on the banister. The cool breeze whipped around us, lifting up a corner of Shiro's loose white shirt. A flash of soft skin caught my attention before it was hidden back from my sight.

"I don't need more friends either. It's fine, Nick. Thank you for letting me use you as a buffer for awkward questions right now. I'm sure I'll get trashed and spill it all later, so it doesn't matter. I shouldn't have asked you to be my fake boyfriend either. I put you in a weird position. Sorry."

"Trust me, that wasn't a weird position."

"Oh no?"

"Not at all." I winked at him. "I can show you a few weird positions."

Shiro chuckled at that. He leaned against the table, looking me up and down. I lifted my chin. There was something about Shiro that hooked me. Was it in that subtle smile he seemed to always wear, even when someone (me) was beginning to grate on his very last nerve? Or was it because I could see something else, glittering even brighter than his smile.

Could it have been that kiss we shared? I had only kissed one man before Shiro, and that had been fueled by a night of tequila drinking and salsa dancing. I could barely remember how that night felt. How his lips had felt, how his tongue tasted.

Not with Shiro. I could still feel his lips against mine, his tongue slipping past mine, his hard body fitting with mine.

And I had liked every damn second of it. Became drunk off it. Thought it had ended way too soon.

Maybe that's why I followed after him. Why I interrupted him and his friends even though Shiro had never dropped anything. The lip balm I handed him had come from my pocket.

And he had accepted it.

"I mean, did you come here by yourself? Do you have any friends here?" Shiro asked.

If only I could answer that honestly.

"Not here, no."

Not anywhere. Luna was a friend, but it became murky when her literal job was taking care of my life. She got paid to be around me twenty-four seven. In fact, I could spot her from the corner of my vision, standing with a cup of water and a straw to her lips, sunglasses and hat on.

Shiro looked me up and down. He crossed his arms, making them look even bigger. The buttons on his shirt pushed apart, giving me a look at his chest, letting me see the curve of muscle, the hint of a nipple.

"Fine, let's be friends."

A smile spread over my face. I switched my hat so that it wasn't throwing a shadow over my face. I had initially freaked out over the fake-boyfriend question as images of me and Shiro holding hands flashed across my face, splattered over every newsstand and grocery store aisle. It would also hit the internet in rapid-fire time, but the Spaniards did love their magazines, and I had no doubt I'd be front-cover material for months.

When I declined the offer, it didn't fill me with any kind of relief. Instead, I had a major what-if moment. The exact kind of thing I was trying to avoid by breaking up with my girlfriend and taking this spontaneous trip.

But friends? That we could definitely do. If, on the small chance there was someone who recognized me on this cruise and was the type to sell photos, then they'd have nothing except for a prince hanging out with his American friends, cruising through the Caribbean for the holidays.

How scandalous could this possibly get?

"So, friend," I said with a grin, "what's one thing I should know about you?" I wanted to get as big a rundown on him as I could before his friends returned and the charades officially began. The air, aside from having a fine ocean mist in it, was also beginning to crackle with excitement. This would be fun; I could already tell. In fact, I was willing to bet that doing anything with Shiro would be fun.

"Well... *friend*. Let's see—I'm twenty-five, I'm a Pisces, I work for a detective agency called Stonewall Investigations. I hate long walks on the beach and love to watch sunsets from places that are high up."

I filed away all that information. "Should a friend know that last one?"

Shiro seemed to have caught himself. He chuckled, his cheeks flashing pink. "Your turn."

"I'm twenty-three. I'm a Virgo. I work with a lot of charities in my spare time. I too hate long walks on the beach, but I also hate heights. So no sunsets from the top of a mountain for me."

Also I'm a closeted prince running away from his life back at home.

"Noted." His face cracked into a smirk. "You're not really into astrology, are you?"

"I'm lucky I even remembered my sign. I thought you were."

Shiro shook his head, the two of us laughing, the sounds mixing well together. "Full disclosure: I am googling whether or not Virgos and Pisces are compatible."

"As friends?"

He nodded, lips pursed. "*Only* as friends." He spoke confidently, but the rosy flush at the base of his neck told me his thoughts went past the boundary of friendship. I imagined what it would feel like to trace the rose-colored flesh with my tongue.

"So you're a detective?" I asked, trying to stop my mind from going rogue and my cock from going rigid.

"Yup. I've been working at Stonewall for three years now. Started right out of college. Got my degree in criminology and interviewed with their Miami branch. They luckily took a risk on hiring me, but I don't think I've made them regret it. I've closed about ninety percent of the cases that come to my desk."

"That's a damn good number."

"It is. I'm proud of it."

I could tell he was by the way he held his chest up when he spoke about his career. There was a glint in his eyes, too, something I didn't often see when people brought up their jobs.

A faint red flag flew up in my brain. If Shiro made a living by uncovering secrets, then he very well could uncover mine. Out of the thousand people on board this ship, of course I had to bump into and fall for the one keen-eyed and incredibly attractive detective.

Except no one's falling for anyone.

"And you?" Shiro asked. "What kind of charities do you work with?"

Thankfully, he didn't dig into my "current" employment. Was he throwing me a bone? I didn't think he'd leave that thread untouched unless he wanted to.

"I work a lot with children," I said, taking whatever bone Shiro gave me. "I have a therapy dog back at home. Eli. A big ol' baby. We go in almost every weekend, if not every other weekend, and we spend time with the kids staying at the hospital. It really brightens up their day, and I feel like Eli gets a lot out of it, too. Hell, I know I do."

Shiro's eyes locked with mine, his brows lifting. "What kind of dog is Eli?"

"A golden retriever," I said, pulling out my phone. It was an unwritten law that whenever one brings up their dog to an interested party, they must be followed up with one of the thousands of cute photos stored in their phone.

I pulled up the most recent. A picture of me and Eli with Patreeka, a little girl who called herself Eli's biggest stan. She had an arm thrown over Eli, her face buried in the side of his fur, his red bandana covering the top of her head. My smile matched Eli's in the photo.

"Oh my freaking God," Shiro exclaimed, grabbing the phone from my hand. "Eli looks like the absolute best dog there is. Literally who the phrase 'good boy' was made for." He smiled a genuine smile, one that spread to me.

"I take it you're a dog person?"

"I am. I'm an animal person. Except for spiders. Or bugs. Any kind of bugs. Then I'm a 'oh fuck no' kind of person."

"Same here," I said, taking back my phone and finding another photo of Eli. This one was of him sitting at the edge of Lake Biscay, directly behind our palace. It was a photo only of Eli, looking back with his tongue lolling out, the lake glowing orange from the light of the setting sun. I showed Shiro, eliciting another high-pitched sound.

"Wow, you have literally the best dog ever. This looks like an ad for organic dog food and blissful retirement all rolled into one cute, fluffy package."

I took back my phone, laughing. Shiro's friends joined

us, Ace coming up behind Shiro and nudging him with a shoulder. I noticed his eyes lingered on me for a moment longer than normal, resurrecting the thoughts of him possibly knowing me. He was distracted by his boyfriend, who pointed out at the bay. Lou and his girlfriend, Elle—or as I secretly named her, Elvira, Mistress of the Text—went over to the railing and took a peek over the deck. I was surprised Elle managed to take her eyes off her phone screen long enough to admire the view. When we had been introduced, I wasn't even sure if I'd get her to look up at me, her shiny black hair almost creating a curtain around her face.

"Oh, look," Shiro said, tapping me with an elbow and pointing up with his chin. I looked up at the ship's towering exhaust stack, a Christmas tree painted onto the front of it, giving the illusion that we would be cruising with a twenty-foot tree on the boat. But that wasn't what had caught Shiro's attention. He was pointing at the white puffs of fake snow that were beginning to fall, propelled out from hidden pipes coming from behind the exhaust stack. The snow filled the air, landing on our foreheads and instantly dissolving. The ship gave a loud and prolonged blast of its horn and started to push forward.

The momentum must have caught Shiro off guard. It wasn't much, but it was enough to make him tip over, falling into my arms. I instinctively opened to catch him, his head landing square on my chest. He looked up at me, saying a soft "thanks," his amber pools catching me as off guard as his trip.

I wasn't sure how long we stayed in that position. Most likely seconds, although it felt like years passed us by.

He regained his footing. I peeled my eyes off him, scared of what I'd do if I kept looking. Scared I would be pushed into reaching out, holding him again. It had felt so natural. A flash of a moment that sealed everything for me. Made me realize exactly what I wanted.

Who I wanted.

"Snow in Miami," Shiro said, speaking so he could be heard over the excited crowd and the wind now beginning to stir around us, whipping the fake snow into swirls as the cruise ship left the bay. "It's a Christmas miracle."

I watched him move his hand through the air, eyes turned to the sky, smile spreading across his face, and I had to agree wholeheartedly with him.

"It sure is."

6 SHIRO BROOKS

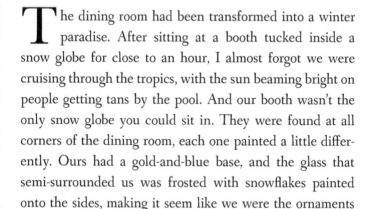

The dining room had been transformed into a winter paradise. After sitting at a booth tucked inside a snow globe for close to an hour, I almost forgot we were cruising through the tropics, with the sun beaming bright on people getting tans by the pool. And our booth wasn't the only snow globe you could sit in. They were found at all corners of the dining room, each one painted a little differently. Ours had a gold-and-blue base, and the glass that semi-surrounded us was frosted with snowflakes painted onto the sides, making it seem like we were the ornaments locked inside.

The rest of the room had touches of the holiday season everywhere you looked. From the employees who looked like Santa's elves with their red-and-green uniforms and droopy hats to the flat-screen TVs that were hung on a couple of different columns, each showing a different holiday film, all of them pulling from the classics. The one that faced us was playing the stop-motion Rudolph film, which happened to be one of my absolute favorites.

"So, Shy, what happened to Mace?" The question had come from across the table, Jada smiling with her bright pink lips. "Did he get nervous about being on a ship for so long? He was always weird about the ocean."

I took a long sip of my Coke, trying to think of some kind of excuse. Nick must have seen me mentally flailing.

"He got sick," Nick answered.

I nod, going along with the story. "He came down with something pretty nasty."

"Well, I should text him, then." Jada grabbed her phone from her sunflower-yellow clutch.

"No! Uh, I mean, he's probably sleeping. He's been sleeping a lot."

"You sure? I feel bad. We haven't talked in months."

"Yeah, I'm sure," I said.

This was unsustainable. I was going to have to come clean. Maybe I should just say it, rip it off like a Band-Aid? "You guys..."

I was interrupted by a loud voice, singing a beat I couldn't recognize right away but one that rang faint bells. The dining room started to grow quiet as the singing grew louder, the original voice joined by more. And then the song started in earnest: "Deck the Halls." I looked around and spotted the Christmas carolers. A group of eight, all different from one another, their voices harmonizing perfectly. The women wore plaid skirts that billowed around them, with deep red velvet jackets and luxurious-looking white scarves. The men wore similar outfits, swapping out the skirts of plaid slacks, the deep reds, royal blues, and emerald greens complementing each other well. They bobbed back and forth, singing and raising their hands, lifting the books they carried up to the ceiling.

And then the music switched up, a beat beginning to play from the speakers and not the carolers. They looked around, all eight of them smiling, and they tossed their caroling books to the side. All eight of them grabbed their outfits and tore their clothes off, revealing bright beach clothes underneath. They busted out into an entire modern dance choreography to a pop version of Mariah Carey's "All I Want for Christmas," the crowd erupting in cheers.

As they performed, Nick and I had gravitated closer to each other. He had to crane over me a little bit to get a good view, and so that provided some cover as to why I could practically lick the inside of his ear if I wanted to.

I restrained myself, content with just smelling his cologne, feeling his warmth against me. I tried reminding myself that he technically said "no" to being boyfriends, so he might not have even wanted me in the first place, but... damn it, I couldn't help myself. Especially not when his hand was now resting on my knee, hidden from sight by the large table that covered us. I glanced around my friend group real quick, seeing that everyone was absorbed with the dancers, who were moving around the dining room and interacting with people now, getting some to get up and dance.

Nick's hand moved, his thumb drawing circles over my bare skin, my shorts having ridden up to about midthigh. I tried controlling my breaths but could feel them start coming in more and more jagged. He squeezed gently, causing a heat to blossom from the point of contact, rising right up to my tightening balls. My thoughts drifted back to our kiss, to his tongue against mine.

I grew harder. To the point that I started hoping none of the dancers came my way and asked to dance with me—

Oh, fuck.

A dancer—a tall guy with short blond hair—locked eyes with me and shimmied over to me, wearing a pair of Christmas tree board shorts. He motioned for me to get up.

"No, that's okay, I'm okay," I said, Nick's hand coming off my knee but my dick still working on a fifteen-second delay.

"Come on!" Lou said, cheering me on from down the booth. "Do it." His girlfriend was finally looking up from her phone, using it to take snapshots of everything happening.

Great, there's going to be photographic evidence of my boner.

"Seriously, I'm a bad dancer," I protested. The dancing caroler took my answer as final and shimmied over to the table next to us, pulling up a grandpa and getting him to twirl his hips to a cheering crowd. Meanwhile, I breathed out a sigh of silent relief.

The show finished shortly after. My blood pressure was still through the roof, and I could feel the sweat that beaded on the nape of my neck.

"I have to run to the bathroom," I said, feeling more than a little flustered with how close Nick and I got under the table. I stood up. Should I have been surprised when

Nick stood up right after me, saying he had to go, too? Maybe. But I wasn't.

I also wasn't exactly upset about it.

We walked through the dining room, passing around a stack of gift boxes that looked like they'd been pulled from a Dr. Seuss movie. They were all kinds of different shapes, wrapped in pastel colors with bold patterns. One item was clearly a trumpet, another a unicorn.

The bathrooms were spared of the holiday decorations. The only touches were in the red and white tinsel that hung above the long mirror, four farm-style basin sinks sitting on top of the marble counter.

Nick was on me in seconds. He started kissing my neck, pushing me back against the counter, his tongue flicking at my skin, his teeth barely pressing down, applying just the right amount of pressure to get me rock hard. I pushed my erection onto him, my hands gliding up and down his back, my head thrown back so I could expose more of my neck to him. A sign of pure submission. He could tear me apart, and I wanted him to. I didn't even care that we were in a public bathroom. Anyone could have walked in, and I would have kept on going, offering a free show with prime seating.

But he stopped. "Let's get in a stall."

He grabbed my hand and started me toward the open stall.

The thought hit me like Grandma getting hit by a herd of reindeer: *Is this a mistake?*

Sure, I could follow Nick into the stall and lose myself to a man who'd walked out of my wildest and horniest fantasies, or I could take a step back and think with the head on my shoulders and not the one below them. Maybe this was right—maybe this was what we should both be doing.

But not yet.

It was my turn to stop. I wanted this in a really bad way. I wanted everything Nick had to offer and more.

I didn't want it here, though. Nor did I want it when we were under friendship pretenses. Those situations never worked out well. Ever. Even if the friendship started as weirdly as ours had. I had to set some kind of boundaries, some ground rules.

"As hard as this is—" I shot a look down between us. "Clearly." We both chuckled. "I've got to bring this up... Damn it, another pun. I didn't even mean that one."

Nick flashed me that perfect grin before kissing me again. Freaking hell, he was making this so difficult. Here I was, literally getting exactly what I had asked Santa for, and yet I was ready to shove it right back up the chimney.

"Ugh," I groaned as I broke from the kiss. "Sorry, but... we've got to set friendship rules. This should clearly be a rule. For friendship. You know?"

"And what's the rule?" Nick's hand went down, past my stomach, rubbing me over my pants and almost causing my eyes to roll backward. "That we have to do this inside of every bathroom? You know"—Nick squeezed, licking his lips—"for friendship."

I parted my lips, ready to succumb. All I had to do was get in the damn stall. Then Nick's hand could be on me without the annoying clothes between us. I could have him, give myself to him. So what if this practical stranger turned out to be a rebound fling for me?

"I can't," I said, the words sounding as if they came from

someone else. Instead of moving away, though, I reached for him, an instinct I couldn't quite place but one that felt loud and forceful. I hooked a thumb through a belt loop on his pants. His hand had moved off me, leaving me with a powerful need that threatened to derail my rules before I even said them out loud.

"This has to be one of the rules," I said. "We have to act like friends. It'll just make things complicated if we don't. There's plenty of guys on this ship; I'm sure we can bump into one under a mistletoe somewhere."

Even though the only guy I wanted under any kind of "toe" is you.

Nick cocked his head and slanted that sexy smile. "What if we can bend the rules when no one's around?"

"I haven't even said what the rest of the rules are yet."

Nick's hands were beginning to roam over my body, slowly traveling up and down my side, fully putting me into a trance. I was like one of those sharks that go comatose when you rub their bellies.

"What are the rules, then?" He was slowly pulling us toward the open stall.

I couldn't think. All I could focus on was the long rod Nick appeared to have smuggled onto the ship in his pants. The outline of his hard dick only deepened that previously mentioned trance.

"Well..." My blood felt ten degrees too hot for my body. "I guess friends with benefits is a thing."

"It sure is."

Nick moved toward me, filling the needless space between us. His evergreen eyes drilled a hole straight down into my core. If he had said to forget friends, let's be fake fiancés, in that moment, I'm pretty sure I would have agreed.

Footsteps sounded toward us, owned by someone merrily singing a holiday tune. The sudden sound made us both leap halfway into the air. We separated, my cheeks dotting with heat as I went over to the sink and ran the water, pretending to have been washing my hands the entire time. Nick did the same at my side. We were conveniently using the counter to hide our erections as we shot quick looks at each other, the both of us having trouble subduing our smiles.

"Hey, you two." I looked in the mirror at a smiling Ace. I should have recognized his voice, seeing as he always took every chance he could to sing. And for good reason, too. He had American Idol written all over him. "Those Cinnabons really make your hands all sticky, don't they?" He went to the open sink, grinning to the both of us through the mirror.

"I haven't had one," I said, turning the water off, confident that I wasn't pitching a tent in my shorts anymore.

"Oh? I thought you got some glaze there."

"Huh? Where?"

Nick watched this exchange. I leaned forward and Ace pointed at a spot on my neck, shiny with Nick's saliva, red with his teeth marks. My eyes went wide. Ace shot me a mischievous look, his eyebrows twitching up as he darted a glance to Nick before turning to the stack of paper towels. "Wow, is it me or is it like twenty-five degrees hotter in here for some reason?"

All right, now Ace was starting to fuck with us. He grabbed some paper towel from the neatly placed stack and dried his hands without taking his eyes off us.

"I think something's wrong with the heater," I said, all three of us knowing damn well nothing was wrong with the temperature control on this ship.

"Right. Anyways! Rex and me are going to go grab some drinks at the bar next to the Elves' Workshop. The rest of the group split up to recharge in their rooms for a bit. Want to come get drinks?"

"Actually," Nick said, stretching. "I think I'm going to head up to my room. Maybe take a power nap."

"Same." I dried my hands, trying to avoid Ace's eagle-like glare as I wiped quickly at my neck. "Going to my room," I clarified, as if I needed to. "For a nap. By myself."

"You guys are going to the ugly-sweater party tomorrow, right?" Nick asked, stopping my runaway train of word vomit in its tracks.

Ace nodded with the excitement of a widely grinning bobblehead stuck on the dashboard of a car with terrible suspension. "Definitely. I've got one of the gnarliest sweaters ever known to mankind. It's really ugly. I can't wait."

"Can't wait to see it." We walked out of the bathroom. Ace threw an arm over my shoulders. He had meteor-sized blue eyes that made him look all the more innocent.

"I'm glad the gang's back together again. Just wish we weren't missing Mason."

"Me too," I said, giving a silent "thank you, baby Jesus" that Mason wasn't here.

Ace left to go get his drinks, and I walked with Nick to the elevators. On the way there, I could tell Nick was thinking about something. His blue eyes seemed to swirl with questions.

"What's up?" I asked as we started to reach the elevator bay.

"I'm just wondering how someone could have let you go."

That caught me by surprise. "Oh, well... yeah. I wonder the same thing," I said with a self-deprecating laugh. "But whatever. Shit happens."

"What kind of shit happened? If you don't mind me asking."

"No, no. That's fine. I guess if we're going to be fake friends, you should know about my real breakup. His name's Mason. He wasn't the greatest, even though I thought he was. I felt like I loved him, but looking back... I don't know. I don't know if what I felt was love." I dropped my head, feeling a heavy weight land on my chest. "It sucks. Basically all he ever did was eat potato chips, watch old movies, and sometimes ask for sex. But I became so used to it, I don't know, I thought it was fine. I felt settled into it. Especially since we had started off as good friends, and I had known him for a couple of years before we started dating. I thought it would be fine, maybe things would click into place. And then, about a month ago, *he* ends up breaking up with me. He joined some crazy Rolling Stones cult. Don't ask. But even then, right before the cult thing, I fully envisioned a future together with him. Sure, it was a shitty future, but it was still a future. And then he dipped." I shook my head and straightened my shoulders. "I don't know. Honestly, it makes me wonder... if I can't keep *that* loser around, then maybe something's wrong with me. Maybe I don't deserve anyone better, if I can't keep them around... I don't know. I'm blabbing."

At the elevator, I pressed on the call button, trying to avoid eye contact with Nick. I felt dumb, saying it all out loud. I felt like I'd been duped. As if time had been stolen from me, even though I knew that wasn't the truth. No one stole anything from me.

"Shy, I've known you for less than twenty-four hours, and I can already confidently say that everything you just said is a steaming pile of bullshit. You absolutely deserve someone who makes you happy, the same way you make others happy." Then, as if to himself: "Everyone deserves happiness."

The elevator doors dinged open. A few passengers stepped out before we stepped in.

"Whatever, it's fine," I said, not wanting to dwell on my shitty dating life. "Let's meet on the deck after our naps. And here, let's swap numbers real quick so we can find each other."

Nick and I traded numbers before I hit the fifth-floor button on the elevator panel. I wasn't sure why, but I had been expecting Nick to be on the same floor as me. Maybe because I kept picturing him in the same room as me.

He pulled out his key card and held it against the black pad before pressing the topmost button. The penthouse equivalent of our cruise ship.

My eyes almost fell out of my skull, but I managed to keep my composure.

Who in the world did I just trade numbers with?

7 NICHOLAS SILVA

I pressed my key card against the pad next to the door. It blinked green. I turned the heavy silver handle and pushed it open, stepping into the living room of my two-bedroom suite. It felt like a large space, with modern furnishings that made me feel as if I were staying inside a floating five-star hotel in the middle of the ocean. The dark leather couch took up the center with two bright blue fabric chairs on the side, facing out toward the wall-to-wall balcony, giving me a breathtaking view of the endless stretch of blue. Christmas decorations dotted the room.

I set my suitcase next to the four-poster bed, a trio of towel animals sitting against the pillow. They were three penguins, with red towels around their necks that made it look as if they all had scarves on.

As I pulled off my socks, I began to really take stock of the situation.

This wasn't how I'd expected to start off my holiday cruise, but I certainly couldn't complain. On the long flight to get here, I imagined how my trip would go. I thought I'd spend it by myself, drinking at the bar or by the pool with a hat and sunglasses on at all times. At night, I'd hop on an app and see if there were any guys on the ship that would be down for some late-night experimenting. I'd have them come to me, and that way, I'd completely avoid the possibility of having anyone photograph the two of us.

The idea had kept me hard for basically my entire flight. I had been turned on enough as it was, and then I bumped into the handsome and confident Shiro Brooks.

More than bumped into him. We had locked lips in an explosive and spontaneous kiss.

I had felt his body push against mine. I could feel him through his shorts, the same way he could probably feel me. And then in the bathroom... I couldn't keep my hands off him. Or my lips. Or the rest of me. I had to have him, not giving a *cruising* fuck about who would walk in through that door. In a matter of hours, I was losing all inhibitions, and it was all because of this exquisite man. He did something to me, something none of my exes had ever done. He lit a fire deep inside my core, one I never wanted to see go out.

My cock twitched, growing rock hard by the time I walked over to the large bathroom. For a flash of a moment, I considered whipping out my phone and calling him, asking him to come up to my suite. I felt comfortable giving him my number since I had left my personal phone back at home, but I knew calling him now might have been too much. So, instead, I'd handle things myself. I unbuttoned my shorts and pulled them over my straining bulge. My briefs followed next, my stiff cock springing up. I gave myself a few strokes, letting my head fall back and my imagination run wild.

But my imagination could only take me so far. I hadn't even got to see Shiro naked. I couldn't picture what he was working with. I couldn't imagine how he'd feel, rubbing himself on me, skin on skin.

I bent down and grabbed my jeans from the floor, and dug in the pocket for my phone.

On my phone, I opened up a private browser and typed in the only address a private browser was used for.

A screen with rows and rows of girls getting pounded in all different directions and positions filled the phone. I didn't tap on any of them. I changed the option at the top, moving the bubble to the "gay" option and away from the "straight" one.

The women were replaced by a screen of naked men, some alone, some together, some in threes and fours and fives. There were straight-passing guys being jerked off with blindfolds on; two beefy men sixty-nineing; a series of guys taking turns fucking a tiny blond twink.

I opened up a few different tabs, choosing as if I had made the line at a five-star fucking buffet. I had spent much of my life hating how much I loved watching two (or more) men go at it, but no more of that bullshit. I wouldn't regret liking what I liked, just as much as a straight person didn't regret liking what they like.

Fuck all that noise.

I leaned against the bathroom counter, the cold marble stinging my ass briefly before I adjusted to it. I played with myself as I watched a video of a guy giving a messy blowjob in the back of a pickup truck. I spit in my hand, bringing it down and stroking, the sound of my wet skin on skin mixing with the loud and sloppy sounds coming from my phone. I dropped my head back and shut my eyes, briefly forgetting about the video, my mind drifting elsewhere, past the phone in my hand. I started to imagine Shy and the way his hand would feel gripped around my cock. How it would feel when it was his spit making me wet. When it was his tongue swirling around the head of my cock.

I let out a primal groan and tugged on my nuts, letting the phone rest on the counter. I didn't pause the video, but my attention was no longer on it. I looked down, admiring myself for a moment, how fucking hard I was, all because of Shiro and his honey-gold eyes. I wanted him looking up at me with those eyes, tears slipping from the corners as he gagged on my size. I stroked harder, my entire body tensing.

But I wanted more. My body had been crying out in a desperate sort of way. I went over to the shower, cock swinging in the air, and turned it on, the showerhead dropping water down in what appeared to be a jungle rain shower. I stepped into the shower, closing the glass door and letting the water fall over me, pushing down on my tense shoulders, my sore neck. Shiro had me wound up. I flexed my muscles, rolled my neck, and then returned my hand down to my hard cock, the water adding a new layer.

This shower was big enough for the two of us with plenty of room to spare. I pictured how Shy would look pressed against the gray-and-white subway tiles, his legs open for me, his cock just as hard as mine. I imagined myself turning around for him, showing him my back, my ass. And then I'd spread for him, letting myself be seen in a way no one else had ever seen me. I'd expose my hole, tease it with a finger for him, until he couldn't take it anymore, until he pressed himself against me, buried himself inside me.

"Fuck," I said into the stream of water. I grabbed the bottle of soap and pumped some onto my fingers. But instead of reaching for my cock, I reached around, sliding my fingers between my crack. I shut my eyes and parted my lips, water dripping down them, and I played with my hole, my cock twitching with every little motion I made. My toes curled against the shower floor. I had only played with my ass a few times before, and all three of those times, I never actually pushed in.

With Shy's eyes emblazoned on my mind, I hooked a soapy finger and applied pressure, feeling the tight ring of muscle relax as I slipped in, a whole new world opening up to me. I explored myself, tentatively at first, moving my fingers in small circles, only going up to the first knuckle.

My cock throbbed up against the falling water. I stepped to the side of the shower, out from underneath the rainfall, finger still inside me. I moaned as I sank deeper, the sound echoing off the glass of the shower. I could feel my inner walls tightening on my finger, almost pulling it deeper. I started to slide in and out, curling my finger, rubbing at my walls, not even touching my cock from fear that I'd blow instantaneously.

"Oh fuck."

I kept going, hitting some part of me that had never

experienced pleasure before, a part of me that shot stars directly across my vision. I stopped finger fucking myself and instead focused on rubbing that spot, feeling myself swollen and aching. I pushed and rubbed, opening my legs, lifting one so that I leaned on a ledge of the soaps. This opened me wider. My balls hung in the air, moving as I started grinding my ass back onto my finger, that spot growing warmer and warmer, my vision tunneling, my muscles tightening and loosening.

An orgasm hit me with the same intensity as a car crash. I hadn't even touched my cock, and it began to explode, shooting come onto the shower wall, rope after rope. My ass clenched tight around my finger with every single shot. Animalistic grunts escaped me. Noises I didn't recall ever making as my balls unloaded, the wall looking like a Jackson Pollock painting by the time I was done.

I pulled my finger slowly out of me, the sensation threatening to knock me off my feet. It didn't help that my knees were shaking after that assault of an orgasm I experienced. Oxygen was difficult to find. I took a few deep breaths. It felt like I'd just been given the key to a secret city, one I only knew about. And it was filled with expensive wine and sex swings and Shiro. Everything I'd ever want.

Under the rainfall I went, dropping my head back, letting the water run down my spent muscles. As the minutes started to tick by, I realized that my hunger wasn't satiated. My cock still hung heavy between my legs, my hole still twitching. As good as fingering myself felt, as great as it was to come without any hands on my dick, I still wanted more.

I wanted Shiro. I wanted him to be spreading my legs apart, feeling me from the inside.

I jerked off one more time, surprised at just how much come I sent down the drain. After toweling off, my dick went back down to manageable levels, only a slight bulge appearing as I pulled on my white shorts. I didn't even bother throwing on a shirt. I went over to the plush bed and dropped down onto the memory foam mattress, the quilt sinking with my weight. The pillows were equally luxurious, feeling as if they had been spun from clouds and silk. I shut my eyes, feeling a deep exhaustion settle into my bones, caressing my muscles.

It wasn't a whole five minutes later when my phone started to ring. I checked, surprised that I even had service. Except it wasn't a phone call; it was a FaceTime call, one that could come in through Wi-Fi.

And it was coming from my mother.

I rolled over on the bed, accepting the call, wondering what in the world she could be calling me about. Normally, she had one of the palace assistants reach out to me if she needed something. A FaceTime call was highly unusual.

Unless...

No. There's no way...

My heart started to pound as I sat up straighter against the headboard, pillow propped against my back. Had pictures gotten out? Was someone in the bathroom?

"Hola, mamá," I said as the call connected, the image slightly pixelated and a lag causing my mom's smile to appear lopsided. She had her brown hair falling down in rivers onto her freckled shoulders, her hair shining even through the pixelated screen.

"Nicholas! Oh, I've missed that handsome face of yours."

"Mamá, I've only been gone three days."

"That's close to ten years in our time. You know that. With how fast things move over here, I feel like I'll be twenty-four years older by the time you get back."

Okay, if she's acting like this, then she hasn't seen any pictures.

I relaxed slightly. "Is everything okay over there?"

"Oh sí, of course everything's okay. What I can't call my son if I'm missing him?"

"You can, I just—"

"Ay, look! Hold on, Nicholas, look who it is. Come over, don't be shy."

Half of my mom's lagged-out face disappeared from the screen, and half stayed on. It didn't take long for her face to be completely replaced by someone else's.

The spontaneous FaceTime call made sense then, and it took everything in me not to tap the End Call button right then.

"Hola," said Catherine Meis, a girl who had been around my family since I could remember, and one whom my mother tried pushing on me almost since as far as I could remember. She was the daughter of the world-renowned Ricardo Meis, the founder of a tech company valued at more than a billion dollars. An entirely different kind of royalty from my family, and one my mother always salivated at the idea of unionizing.

I didn't have time or patience for this. Leave it to my mother to try and hook me up with someone only days after I announced my breakup.

"Sorry, Catherine," I said, cutting things off before they could escalate, "I've got to go. The ship is, uh, rocking pretty bad."

She looked confused, probably seeing that I was standing quite comfortably on two feet, no rocking in sight.

I hung up the call before my mom could get back on. With an exhale, I threw my phone onto the bed and continued to get ready, trying to forget about the drama that awaited me back home. I had to let it all go. I had to focus on the here and now.

Which happened to be very easy to do when I started picturing Shiro again, here on the bed, lying down and waiting for me, like a Christmas gift I had to unwrap with my teeth.

Annnd, I'm hard again.

8 SHIRO BROOKS

Silver and red fairy lights twinkled above us, strung up with invisible wire between the classic lampposts that lined the cobbled street. An instrumental version of "Jingle Bells" played through invisible speakers tucked inside holly bushes potted in beautiful white vases, their dark green leaves making the bright red berries pop. We sat in a circle around a table set on the deck, the ocean stretching out around us in every direction. We could see the moon glitter off the dark water as the cruise ship cut through the peaceful waters.

Lou and his girlfriend—who I'd only *just* learned was named Elle, and that was because her phone's battery had died and she was forced to join in the conversation—were sitting next to me, both of them sipping on their candy cane rum drinks. Jada was retelling an animated story of the time

Lou and I got locked out of our dorm and had to sneak up the side of the building to slip in through the window. Lou only made it up to the second floor, but I climbed my way up to the fifth.

"I still don't know why you didn't just call me," she said, laughing after she got to the part where I ended up going into the wrong window.

"We should have," I answered. "It would have saved everyone a lot of trouble." I started blushing remembering the two frightened faces who had looked up from their fellatio marathon to see a virtual stranger crawling in through the window. To make matters all the worse, this had happened after we went to an "anything but clothes" party, so I was wearing a makeshift top and bottom created from holiday ribbons. I looked batshit crazy.

Thankfully, I had known Paul and Manny after I helped them move into the dorms. They were both incredibly drunk, which helped the situation. They threw on boxer shorts and helped me inside.

"And we still had to wake up the RA." Lou shook his head, a smile lighting up his face.

"The A-B-C party was worth it, though," I said, spotting Ace walking toward us from across the deck. He had a spring in his step. Rex walked close behind him, same spring. I was surprised to see another figure with them.

Nick. He lacked the spring.

They walked around the packed tables, everyone wanting to sit on the deck for the first night out at sea. Ace waved and twirled as he came over to us. I noticed Rex eating him up with his eyes. It reminded me of the way Nick had looked at me inside the bathroom.

Heat flashed across my chest, down into my crotch.

"Hey, guys," I said, moving my chair so that there was space for the three of them. Nick sat next to me, looking as good as ever in a simple white T-shirt and navy blue shorts. I noticed a woman walking toward the table, one I had spotted a couple of times already. At first I thought one of us had dropped something, but she walked past us, going over to the railing and leaning against it, her hat almost getting blown off by a sudden gust of wind.

"How were your naps?" Lou asked, looking at Ace and Rex, who had clearly done everything except nap.

"Wonderful," said Ace, his green eyes glittering. Rex, a man who lived up to his name with big burly arms and a jaw that looked strong enough to bite a tree in half, also had a glitter in his gaze.

"Oh, these two napped *reallll* hard," Jada said, brow arched, straw in her mouth. She took a big sip as Ace burst into giggles.

"Yes, if by nap you mean Rex pummeled me inside of the massive tub in our room."

"Ace!" Jada exclaimed, slapping playfully at his chest. Rex adopted a cocky little smile but said nothing. I had a feeling he was used to Ace's big mouth as much as we were. "Nice," she followed up in a stage whisper.

I wondered what Nick was thinking about all this. He smiled and laughed and dropped a couple of jokes. He seemed comfortable. He also didn't need to be here. Maybe I should have been more forceful in turning him away. I remember feeling pissed off that he wouldn't take up my crazy plan on the spot, and I could see how crazy that all was in hindsight, but still, the frustration toward him all disappeared in a flick of his butterfly-winged eyelashes.

And now he was hanging out with me and my friends as if he were one of the originals. I had to remind myself that he was only pretending to know me for my friends, and for what? So that I could avoid a couple minutes of awkward conversation?

Or because he just wanted to be around me? Like I wanted him to.

"So," Lou said, sitting back in his seat, putting an arm around his girlfriend, who was beginning to look more and more lively as time passed. I wondered if maybe she was a vampire and needed the moonlight to charge up her batteries. "How do you know Mason, Neal?"

Ah, fuck.

We never really got a chance to solidify any backstories in this "fake" friendship of ours. We had only talked about ourselves and then got too busy rubbing up on each other to talk about anything else. Which I totally didn't mind, but it made moments like these complicated.

"From work," Nick said.

Fuuuuck.

He had no idea what Mason worked as. He couldn't have predicted the literal grave he dug himself.

"Oh snap," Lou said. "Wait, so do you embalm bodies, too? Or are you involved more on the business side?"

Nick almost spit out the beer he was drinking. To his credit, he covered it well with a follow-up cough. I had to steer this ship in a completely opposite direction because Lou had set us straight toward an embalmed iceberg.

"Neal was talking about Mason's last job," I said, feeling

weird using Nick's middle name, as if I'd known him for years already and gotten used to calling him by his first. "His dog-walker job."

"Right. Exactly."

I noticed Ace shoot a suspicious look toward us, but I ignored it.

"So is that what you do now?" Jada asked. Her boyfriend had ended up getting seasick and stayed inside their room to try and sleep it off.

"Not exactly," Nick answered. "I do a lot of work with my therapy dog, but that's not my full-time job, no."

I flashed back to the elevator and how Nick took it all the way to the top level. He definitely wasn't a dog walker, I could be sure of that.

"All right, you know what, everyone put your fingers up." Jada held her hands in the air, all ten fingers out. "We're playing Never Have I Ever."

"Oh lordy," said Ace, who eagerly put his hands up. I had a feeling he'd take off his sandals and throw his toes up in the air, too, if he could.

I turned to my side, trying to give Nick a look that said *you could go*. And if the look didn't do it, I threw a nod toward the doors that led into the ship. I didn't want him feeling like he was some kind of hostage. He could go have drinks by the bar and hop on Grindr if he wanted to. I was sure he could find a seaman or two who would be more than willing to go up with him to the penthouse suite.

Nick subtly shook his head and put his hands up, smiling as he did it. He looked at my hands. "Come on, let's play."

There was my confirmation. Nick was here because he

wanted to be. I put my hands up, joining the circle of wiggling fingers.

"All right, so to recap rules, if you've done something that's talked about, put your finger down. The one with the least amount of fingers wins both in the game and at life!" Jada clapped her hands and started us off, going the nonsexual route first by saying she'd never skydived. I remembered playing this game in college, always being one of the people with the most fingers in the air. I had been pretty innocent back then.

Ace was next. I expected another softball question but was quickly reminded that with Ace, one could never expect anything.

"Never have I ever... been double-fisted."

Lou snorted at that, and Jada laughed out loud. I put my head in my hands, laughing into my palm.

"What? I couldn't say just one fist, since... well. Yeah. Who's put their fingers down?" Ace looked around the table, his innocent eyes bright with the moonlight and twinkling fairy lights. "Y'all wanted to play, right?" He laughed as Rex kissed the side of his head. Ace seemed to have melted instantly at the touch, slinking sideways into Rex, practically climbing onto his lap.

"All right, I'm next," I said, still holding up all ten fingers. I noticed Nick had his fingers up, too, leading me to believe he'd never jumped out of a plane or had two fists up his ass, and definitely not at the same time.

So, he wasn't a risk taker. Duly noted.

"Never have I ever..." I tossed around a few statements in my head, not knowing how dirty to go with my turn. I looked around at my group of friends and knew I couldn't pump the brakes now. After Ace's fisting fiasco, I figured I had to keep the sex ball rolling. "Never have I ever gotten my salad tossed."

"Oh, Shy! Seriously?" Ace said, sitting back up and dropping a finger.

Jada put her finger down, too, looking at me with some pity. "Mason needs to step it up."

"He sure does," I said half-heartedly. Next to me, Nick quietly dropped a finger, and my entire body turned into a bundle of live wire. I tried so damn hard not to picture Nick bent over, hands on his cheeks, spreading himself wide open so someone could eat his ass.

Annnnnd, of course, it was the only thing my brain could now focus on.

Nick was up next. He sucked on his lower lip, doing even more to my body than I thought I could handle. I started to pump my legs together, which made me focus on the way my dick was growing harder by the second.

"Never have I ever had sex with a man."

I had to work to keep my jaw from dropping. Ace and Rex and Jada all put their fingers down. I followed, working on a five-second delay.

Assumptions. The worst things to make, and I had made them. With the way Nick had kissed me, and how he handled me when we were alone, it had me automatically assume that he knew his way around a guy's body.

Next was Elle, who said that she'd never had sex in a car before. We all dropped fingers for that one. The game continued, the group of us giggling like kids stumbling on bad words in a magazine. At one point, I looked out to the jet-black ocean and realized how lucky I felt. When Mason and I broke up, I was sure my entire trip would be ruined. I thought I'd turn into a sailing grinch, locked up in his room and avoiding all kinds of good memories.

Instead, the complete opposite happened. Fun was being had, and memories were being made, all while we sailed on a five-star cruise ship decked out for the holidays.

And, not to forget the star on top of the tree, there had been the practically serendipitous meeting of the mysterious and oh-so-freaking-handsome Nick. If I had boarded this ship with Mason, then I had a strong feeling Nick and I never would have even exchanged words. Now, he was sitting next to me, his knee bumping into mine, lingering, hidden by the table. At one point, his entire leg pressed against mine. There was a palpable heat that rolled off him. It scrambled me like eggs poured onto a hot skillet.

The game came to an end without too many more realizations. I wasn't sure if my poker face could handle any more bombs coming from Nick. Once all hands came down, yawns started to take their place.

"All right, guys." Ace rested his head on Rex's shoulder, which I feel could have doubled as a helicopter landing pad. "I think we're heading to bed."

"Same," Lou said, stretching his arms. Elle seemed like she was about ready to run a marathon, but she didn't say anything, just nodded and stood up as the rest of us did. Nick stretched, too, his arm lifting over my head, his intoxicating scent drifting in my direction. My knees shivered. I suddenly felt as awake as Elle. Like I could run a marathon, but only if it was with Nick and only if we were naked and only if we weren't actually running but fucking.

We walked as a big group to the elevators. Before

getting in, Nick said his goodbyes to us, saying he was going to write a quick email. He stepped aside after we all said our good-nights, walking toward the atrium where he took a seat on one of the benches. I was tempted to follow him, to say that maybe I also needed to write an email, and that we could write our emails together.

Possibly naked.

But no, I didn't follow. I figured that would just bring up more questions than I already had bubbling inside me. And besides, I was feeling pretty exhausted. A good night's rest didn't sound like a terrible idea.

We rode the elevators up to our floors and said good night to each other as we all separated. Ace was *literally* carried down the hall by Rex, his giggles falling behind him like a trail of horned-up breadcrumbs.

With a yawn I unlocked my room. Inside, I stripped down to my briefs and crawled into bed, exhausted after a full day of reunions, fake friendships, and bathroom hookups. I could hardly believe that I'd been on this cruise for less than a day. It felt like we had already gone halfway across the world with everything that had happened.

In bed, I grabbed my phone and started to mindlessly scroll through my usual apps. A couple of times, I'd find myself thinking about Nick and what he was up to in his room.

In his penthouse suite. Jesus. Who the hell did I end up kissing? What if he was some kind of celebrity I didn't recognize? Those girls at the start of the cruise seemed to have thought he was someone... maybe he was?

Or maybe I was just overthinking things. He was just a super-hot guy with a ton of money. Not everyone who was rich had to be famous. Who knew, maybe he had won this trip in some holiday contest? There were a hundred different possibilities, and I wasn't about to keep myself up trying to ponder them all.

I continued to scroll, a couple of steamy GIFs popping up on my timeline. It was clearly the late-night social media crowd. I paused on one particularly hot GIF, feeling a familiar heat rise inside me. It was of two men kissing, one of them in gray sweats and another in black gym shorts. I slipped a hand under the heavy covers and adjusted my growing boner.

Before I clicked on the account, deciding that I had plenty of steam to blow off, I accidentally scrolled down on the page, losing the sexy GIF.

Determined, I flicked my thumb, the different tweets blurring together. The scrolling stopped on a picture, except it wasn't the photo I was looking for. I was about to keep scrolling but stopped. Something about the photo looked incredibly familiar.

I focused, realizing I knew exactly where the photo was taken and when.

Mainly because I was in the center of the frame, Nick holding me, his back turned to the camera, the deck of the cruise ship having been filled as we were leaving port. It had been the briefest of moments. I had fallen into Nick's arms, and he had caught me. The entire thing happened in a matter of seconds, and yet, in this photo, it made it seem like I was being held as we took off on our damn honeymoon, Nick's arms wrapped around me tight.

"What the..."

Why was there a photo of me and Nick? And why did it

have close to... holy goat cheese balls, why did it have *ten thousand* likes?

I read the caption next: Was the Prince of Spain spotted with Mystery Man on a Holiday Cruise?

Prince of... the Prince of... Prince.

What in the holy fuck. No, this had to be a mistake. He must have just resembled the guy. He probably had one of those faces, the ones that make you throw a second glance only to then realize he was just another hot guy in the crowd and not someone from a royal family.

"This is freaking crazy."

I started to read the comments. Most of them were in Spanish, which I had a decent grasp on but still needed to tap on the "translate" button so I could make sure I wasn't hallucinating.

"That is our prince, I'd recognize his back anywhere."

"No way. Prince Nicholas isn't gay!"

"Prince Nick is an LGBTQ icon, wow."

"The prince can't be gay, NO."

"Can he come cruise with me, ayyy."

I felt nauseous and it wasn't because of the ship's motion. This couldn't be real. They had to be mistaken. Either that or this was some elaborate prank. Jada had always been into pranks—maybe she'd decided to go all out for our reunion.

I switched out of the app and opened up my absolute best tool as a detective. One I couldn't go a day without, even when I wasn't on the clock:

Google.

There, I typed in "Prince of Spain." I didn't hit Search right away. My thumb hovered over the button. I allowed my thoughts to drift for a brief moment into fantasy land. What if... if he really was the prince of Spain? I had shared a kiss with a prince, and it had been one of—no, no, let's be real here, it had been the *best* kiss of my entire damn twenty-five years of existence, and I'd put money down that it would remain as the best kiss for the duration of said existence.

I took a breath and pressed Search, sitting up on the bed, finding only articles at first and seeing a photo of the prince as a child.

But the name of that child... Nicholas Silva.

Nicholas.

Holy mother-princing shit.

More recent photos popped up, and any kind of doubt I had disappeared. There were shots of Nick leaving bars, restaurants, clubs. Always holding a girl's hand, a stunning woman with dark black hair that fell down in a sheer curtain toward the small of her back. Then there were the articles talking about their recent break-up, and the shockwaves it caused when the news hit.

Nick was freaking royalty? And I was just photographed in his arms?

Oh *wow*, was this Christmas turning out to be packed full of surprises already.

9 NICHOLAS SILVA

I woke up in great spirits. The sun streamed in through the windows that lined the wall next to the bed, breaking in through the corners of the blackout curtain that covered the balcony door. I half expected to hear a chorus of birds chirping before I remembered that we were miles out in the middle of the ocean, where I'd hear dolphins chirping before birds. I stretched underneath the covers, running my hands down my body, giving my morning wood a squeeze. I normally slept naked, and last night was no exception, although my constant boner for Shiro made it a little harder than usual.

I rolled over on the bed and grabbed my phone from the white nightstand. I had set it facedown and on night mode so that no notifications woke me up during the middle of the night.

First I woke to messages from Luna, telling me "I had to call her immediately." Then followed messages from my mother telling me to *also* call her immediately.

Before I could dial back either of them, my phone started to vibrate as I got a FaceTime call.

From my father.

What in the world had happened? I got out of bed and quickly threw on a shirt and boxers before accepting the call, moving over to the balcony where I looked out at the sky-blue ocean as the call connected.

"Nicholas, where are you?"

My father, a man who carried the crown and never let the crown carry him, had a demeanor that could scare a lion. Growing up, I learned that his facade didn't extend too deeply. He had a soft core underneath the hardened exterior, something not many were aware of. It allowed me to challenge him, to push at the boundaries he had set. I learned that even though he was the king, he was still my father.

"I'm on a cruise," I said, sleep still clouding my thoughts. "Is everything okay? ¿Donde esta mamá?"

"Your mother is fine. I'm getting told that there are photographs circulating. Is there anything you need to tell me? Anything we need to handle?"

"Photos?"

Instantly, I assumed the worst. Someone had snapped a shot of me and Shiro swapping spit. The secret was out. Everyone was going to know. I wanted to pass out, but I steadied my legs and focused on finding a way out of this.

"Well, one photo. But knowing my son, I have a feeling there could be more."

"I haven't seen anything."

My father turned his phone. He had been sitting in the study, the wall of books behind him now being replaced by the screen of his computer. On the center was the photo, and if I didn't catch myself, I would have breathed out a sigh of relief.

Yes, it was a photo of Shiro and me, but my back was turned to the camera and it was difficult to tell it was me. And, although Shiro was in my arms, I could still see plenty of ways to spin it, one of which happened to be the truth: "My friend fell and I caught him. Is that why you're FaceTiming with me as if the palace caught on fire?"

"It will catch fire if this turns out to be more than just a friend catching another one, Nicholas."

A flare of anger rose inside me. I should have done it. Should have just come out right then and there. My father must have sensed something, or he wouldn't be so worried about other photos leaking. He had to have some kind of idea.

And still, I kept my mouth shut.

"Nick," my father said. "You left us here having to deal with stories upon stories, of how you broke Cristella's heart. Devastated her. There had been rumors of marriage, and now there's rumors of you being gay. How am I supposed to handle this?"

The word cut through me like a sharpened blade. He had said it with such a toxic disdain.

Gay.

Exactly what I was, and what my father dreaded to hear.

"You can handle it. You're the king."

My father rubbed the bridge of his nose. He looked out the window to his left, his eyes catching the light. I saw something reflected in them. Was it pain?

"Nicholas..."

"All right, I've got to go." *And figure out who the fuck is leaking photos.*

I didn't let my father get in another word. I clicked the call off, dropping my head against the glass door of the balcony. Part of me wanted to cry. I wanted to crack like an egg and let the tears flow like yolk. This was torture. Why couldn't I just have said it then and there? *Father, I'm gay. The crown can fucking deal with it, but guess what? Your son can't. Your son can't keep getting eaten up like he's been infested with termites.*

I held it together. This wasn't the time to break. I took a deep breath and went to my suitcase. I changed into a pair of light-blue boardshorts and a black T-shirt. I slipped my hat back on and grabbed the sunglasses, too, the circular lenses hiding much of my face.

With my impromptu disguise in place, I left my room. Luna, the guardian angel that she was, had been sitting in the hallway, standing up the second she saw me.

"Nick, did you see?"

I nodded, lips pursed. The hall was empty, but I still couldn't trust anything. Not after it was confirmed that someone on this ship knew who I was and who to send photos to.

"I need to have a chat with my friend," I said, walking to the elevator bay. "Keep your eyes peeled, Luna."

"I will, Nick."

We got onto the elevator, falling silent when someone

else joined us, the woman smelling strongly of coconut sunblock. She smiled pleasantly as the glass elevator took us down. I mustered up a smile back even though my insides all felt like they'd been replaced with jelly.

How the hell was I going to tell Shiro this? That I was actually the closeted prince of Spain and I now needed his help to find out who was sneaking pictures of me on this ship? His mind was going to blow. Would he be upset? Would he be scared? After the immense amount of fun I'd been having with him, I certainly didn't want to scare him away.

Fucking hell.

If I were out and proud, I wouldn't have to worry about scaring Shiro away. I could have been truthful with him from the start. I could have prevented this entire mess by just living my truth instead of living this fucked-up lie.

The elevator opened on Shiro's floor. I stepped out, Luna following. She stayed a close distance behind me but hung back even farther when I reached Shiro's door. She gave me a thumbs-up when I threw a glance her way. I had a feeling that, out of everyone on this planet, Luna had known me better than most. In her eyes, I saw recognition. She knew the photo wasn't an accident or I wouldn't have been freaking out so much about it. I had a feeling she understood the storm that raged inside me on a daily basis. She tipped her straw hat back down on her face, concealing her eyes just as Shiro's door opened.

"We've got to talk," I said.

"Oh, trust me, I know."

"You... know?"

"I know."

I drew my brows together. "You know... what?"

"Get inside," Shiro said, grabbing my wrist and pulling me into his room. He shut the door, his back falling against it. He looked like the definition of a snack, wearing black shorts that ended midthigh, hugging his muscular legs. His shirt was a black V-neck with pink writing scrawled over the chest saying the date and city of the Ariana Grande concert he'd bought the shirt at.

"Mind the mess," Shiro said, motioning at the suitcase sitting on his bathroom floor, clothes spilling out of it. "I don't have a royal cleaning crew."

"So... you do know."

"That you're a freaking prince? Yes, I figured that out last night."

"How?"

Shiro pulled out his phone and showed me the tweet he had stumbled on.

"And then I did some googling. It wasn't that hard."

"Fuck."

"Yeah, that's a good way to put it." Shiro grabbed his phone back and walked to his bed. He sat on the edge of it, looking at me as if I were a Rubik's cube he was trying to solve. His eyes raked over me, looking me up and down and up again. "I can't believe it." He said it to himself, but I still heard.

"Shy..."

"The prince of Spain."

"Please, just call me Nick."

"Okay." He slanted his lips into a smirk. "Prince Nick."

I rolled my eyes. "Just Nick."

"I'll think about it."

I went over to the table that was set against the light brown wall. His balcony curtains had been drawn open, giving us a view of the sun glittering off the blue waters. I took a seat, facing him. "I would have said something before you found out this way."

"Really?" Shiro asked. His walls were going up. I could tell in the way he sat, his legs angled away from me, his hands in a tight fist on his lap.

"I swear it. I would have told you, I just needed a little bit more time. This vacation was supposed to give me an escape I've been needing. So I'm sorry I wasn't very forthcoming about my title, I just haven't been wanting to think about it much."

"Isn't that a little hard when, you know, you're a *freaking* prince?"

"I'm coming to learn it's harder than I thought."

Shiro let out an exasperated breath. "This is crazy."

"It is." I latched on to that statement like a bass on a worm-wiggling hook. "It's crazy how intense our chemistry is. How it's exploded in a matter of hours. It's crazy how I haven't been able to stop thinking about you, even with the threat of being outed by some dickhead with a camera phone. For the first time in my life, I'm beginning to think, 'fuck it.' And that's what's so fucking crazy about all this."

Shiro looked to me, his liquid-gold eyes catching the sunlight just right, lighting them up as if he had two small stars tucked behind his pupils. "I haven't been able to stop thinking about you either."

"That has to mean something. I've never met someone who's done that to me."

Shiro chewed on the inside of his cheek before speaking. "Me neither."

I stood up, moved to the bed. Shiro didn't move away. He did the opposite, opening up to me, as if the distance was the only thing that had been bothering him. He turned toward me, his hands moving to either side of him, his fingers brushing against mine. The air between us crackled and popped.

It was Shiro who broke first, who pushed through the electric force field that separated us. His lips found mine, crushed against them. His hands came up to my head as I took his tongue into my mouth, let it dance with mine. There were no cameras, no prying eyes. Just me and Shy, sharing a kiss that sealed our fates, even if neither of us knew that yet.

When we broke for air, Shiro's eyes locked with mine, his breath tickling my lips.

"Crazy," he said again, before I claimed him with my mouth.

Our kiss was one that lasted, both of us exploring the other with our lips locked and our hands roaming. I rubbed his hard chest over his shirt, while his hand explored my back, slipping under my shirt and sliding over my skin. We kissed and groped and let the worries we were feeling dissolve into the air, rising with the steam that swirled from the both of us.

Three hard knocks on the door interrupted us. Shy's eyes went wide. He got up and tiptoed over to the door, peeking through the peephole. He turned back to me and mouthed out, "Ace" before motioning to his open bathroom. I stood and went inside, silently shutting the door.

I could hear Shiro greet his friend, a slight rawness to his voice.

"Shy, get out of bed and come to the ugly Christmas sweater party!"

"Is that where everyone's going? I thought it was tonight."

"It's an all-day thing. We want to get some day-drinking in. I've been texting you," Ace said, his voice getting louder. Wait, had he come inside?

I started to panic.

"Like my sweater?" Ace sounded as if he were just outside the bathroom door. I heard jingling.

"I can't even believe someone knit that thing," Shiro said with a laugh, one that sounded nervous. "All right, well, let me get ready, then. Go downstairs, I'll meet you guys. It's in the igloo room, right?"

"Yup," Ace said, sounding almost as if he were inside the bathroom with me. My heart was beating so loud I was scared he would hear it through the door. "Let me just use your restroom real quic—"

"No!" Shiro must have pressed his body against the bathroom door because it shook. I leaned against the counter, feeling as if the gig was about to be up. The bathroom was tiny, and there were zero escape routes, unless I pushed out the small round window and jumped down into the sea.

"I, um, well, you don't want to go in there right now."

"Ooookay... Shy, do you still have that stomach thing? Where you had that special doctor's note in college for? The one where you poo—"

"No!" Shiro shouted again. I had to swallow down a

laugh. "I don't have any stomach thing. Stomach is actually better than ever. The best. Now go. Like *now*."

I could hear shuffling toward the door and then the door shutting. Moments later came a knock on the door and Shiro saying, "It's safe."

I walked back out. Shiro's cheeks were flushed pink. "That was close. Sorry for the scare."

"It's all right," I said, shutting the bathroom door. "Glad your stomach's doing better."

"Okay, don't."

I laughed and sat back down on the edge of the bed. Shiro sat, too, his face cracking into a smile.

"I should start getting ready for the party," Shy said, his hand on my thigh. "Before Ace comes barging back in here."

"Mind if I tag along?"

"What? Yeah, of course. I just... you don't have to always hang around me. Maybe, after the photo, maybe it's best we don't hang out too much... at least in public?"

"Is that what you really want?" I was suddenly scared of what his answer would be.

"No. Not at all."

"Good. I don't want that either." I sighed and ran a hand through my hair, feeling the frustration take hold. "I don't want to hide. Ever again. But... I'm also not ready to fully come out. I can't."

"It happens on your time, Nick. Don't let some sneaky-ass paparazzi take that from you."

The ship rocked gently, left to right. We were supposed to spend the entire day at sea, and then tomorrow we would drop anchor at Princess Cays. I had planned on spending the day by myself, sipping rum out of coconuts on some sandy beach, but those plans were quickly vanishing as I realized all I wanted to do was spend time with Shy.

"I won't," I said, digging fingers into the tense muscle between my shoulder and neck. "When did you know? That you were gay?" This was the first time I'd ever spoken about this with anyone. With every word I said, another shackle fell loose from my body.

"Probably since the sixth grade when I tried to kiss Tommy Campanella by the swings after I'd just been asked to a Sadie Hawkin's dance by the girl who'd been crushing on me since I could remember."

"That would do it," I said, chuckling.

"How about you?" he asked. It felt like Shy had just handed me a key. A question I'd never been asked before, and one I so desperately needed to answer.

The floodgates had been opened.

"I've always known... I've always felt a pull. I went to an all-boys school and never quite got along with anyone, and that's because I felt so out of place. While everyone talked about the girls they'd want to date, I was picturing myself with my classmates. Never speaking about it, and painfully reprimanding myself in the beginning for even letting myself think the things I'd been thinking. It was shitty, but it seemed to have worked for a while. I started dating girls, and the thoughts, they never disappeared, but they did subside." I shook my head and took a deep breath, feeling like even my lungs were trembling with emotion. "Only for a little while, though. I couldn't keep my true self down, no matter how hard I tried. I remembered the day I met the American president's son, and it had just been the two of us, and I had felt something spark. Nothing happened between us and he's married now with two kids, but still, it had all resurfaced that day. I wondered if maybe I was bi, but I realized I couldn't find any romantic feelings for any of the women I'd ever been with, and the sex didn't really do it for me either. I would look at openly gay men and find myself feeling jealous. Hatefully so. I wanted what they had so badly. And I thought I'd never get it... Shit. I still feel like I might not get it."

"You will get it, Nick. You deserve it, just as much as everyone else. Just by saying all this out loud, you're one step closer."

"It does feel like I am. Like I got this massive weight off my chest."

I noticed a glint of something in Shy's brown eyes before he wiped it away. "You don't have to feel the weight again. Even if a picture or two leaks, you have keep that weight from settling back."

"On that note... I actually need your help. You said you worked at a detective agency, right?"

"Mhmm."

"Well, I need to find out who took and leaked that photo. I need to stop them from sending anything else they might have. Or from taking any more of us. Because, trust me, I don't plan on staying far from you."

Shiro's brows scrunched together. "That sounds almost like you're ready to throw someone overboard."

"No, never." I shook my head. "I've dealt with this before. The paparazzi, the ones who scrape from the bottom of the barrel, they can always be bought. I have the bank account of an entire crown behind me. I can make sure no more photos of me get out."

His expression shifted from one of apprehension to something bordering on excitement.

"All right," he said, clapping his hands together and sitting up a little straighter. "Let's figure out who the hell is snapping shots of us."

"So you'll help?"

"I'll take your case, Prince Nick."

I smiled. "Perfect." I kissed him then, as if I were unable to stop myself, like the excitement had come over me in a tidal wave.

"I'll keep my eyes open for anyone suspicious, but let me ask you a couple of questions so I can figure out what I'm looking for."

"Shoot."

He walked over to the bedside table and grabbed the black leather notebook sitting next to a miniature Christmas tree, shiny red ornaments hanging off its tiny branches. "Did you come on the ship with anyone?" he asked, walking back to the bedside, pen and notebook now in hand.

"The head of my security team, yeah. Her name's Luna. She's been watching me for the last fifteen years, though. I trust her with my life. Quite literally."

I could tell Shiro still had a few question marks over his head. He wouldn't be a good detective if he didn't.

"What's she look like?"

"Tall, with short brown hair. A pointed nose and a kind smile. Blue-gray eyes... Actually, forget it, I'll just introduce you two."

"Perfect. I'd like to ask her a couple of questions, too." He jotted something down, clicking his tongue to the roof of his mouth. "Did either of you tell anyone about this trip? Was it planned way in advance?"

"We bought the tickets weeks ago and told no one. I wanted it to be as quiet as possible. Even my father didn't know, which is a rare occurrence."

"And you haven't recognized anyone on the ship so far, right?"

I shook my head. "No one. Besides Luna of course." I rubbed my chin, my stubble scratching an itch on my finger. "Is this an impossible task? Did I just ruin your vacation?"

Shy huffed out a laugh. "Are you kidding? You've made this vacation, Nick. I'm going to figure out who's on this ship and leaking photos of you. That's beyond fucked up. You should be able to live without worrying over who's profiting from rumors and unsolicited photos of you." He pursed his lips into a tight smile. "And me."

"Thank you, Shy."

"Of course."

I kissed that smile of his, kissed him until he said we needed to go down to the sweater party before Ace knocked down the door SWAT-style. I didn't want to go anywhere, just wanted to keep kissing him until we ended up as a tangle of arms and legs and tongues. I never wanted to leave the confines of this room, just wanted to stay with Shy, exploring his body after shedding off all our clothes, cruising into Christmas with his naked form against mine, not worrying about the outside world for a single second.

That sounded like it would end up being one hell of a holly jolly Christmas.

10 SHIRO BROOKS

The ugly Christmas sweater party was popping. The Frosty Ballroom had been packed from wall to wall with cruisegoers wearing their ugliest of sweaters. The grand room had been transformed so that it looked like we were inside of a large igloo. The walls had been covered in big, opaque bricks that looked like they were carved from ice blocks, blue and white light shining from behind them, casting an icy glow on the party. The temperature also reflected the setting; the air-conditioning must have been working on overtime to cool down the huge space. There was a lot of dancing and drinking and eating, along with a corner that had an assortment of different board games and card games people could play. It didn't help that the ship appeared to be going through some rough waters and was slightly choppier than usual, but the drinks and good company minimized any discomfort.

Nick and I sat next to a Christmas tree, which looked fake but still gave off the fresh pine scent that always teleported me to the holiday season. It was decorated in blue and silver ribbons and balls, a bed of golden gift boxes wrapped up and piled underneath.

None of it really mattered, though, and that was all because I could hardly take my eyes off the man sitting in front of me. A man whose secrets had been unraveled and who now felt even more surreal than before. I had initially thought Nick looked princely, making him feel like he had waltzed onto the ship after walking straight out of a fairy tale.

I had no idea that Nick actually *was* a prince. And now I wondered if there actually *was* a fairy tale.

If things weren't complicated before, they sure as hell were now.

I couldn't continue staring at him forever, though. One: because that was creepy as hell, and I wasn't here about to scare off the man of my dreams by acting like Krampus. And two: I found myself back on the job even though vacation was far from over.

I didn't mind it. I loved my job, and I loved to help people with their problems, even when those problems quite literally fell on my lap. I wasn't about to tell Nick I couldn't help him figure out who was leaking the photos because I was off the clock. So I would occasionally peel my eyes off Nick and his perfect princely jawline and scan the crowd, trying to spot any lingering cruisegoers, anyone who had their gaze in our direction for too long. I already clocked one lady wearing a vomit-green sweater with two elves holding hands on the front who angled her phone toward us a couple of times already, and then there was a man in a maroon sweater with silver tinsel attached randomly around it, who I had caught staring on multiple occasions.

I filed them away in my memory, noting the woman's halo of orange hair and the man's bald head and crooked-toothed smile. I was going to keep my eye on them, same way they appeared to be doing to us.

"Hey, Nick, when you get a chance, stretch to your left and look at the man in the red sweater. Do you know him?"

Nick put his arms in the air and gave a convincing yawn as he stretched, twisting his body so he looked in the direction I asked. But, just as he did it, the man turned and moved behind the large Frosty the Snowman cake sitting on a tall table against the wall.

"Who?" Nick asked, finishing his stretch.

"Forget it, he moved."

"Think he was taking photos of us?"

"I've just spotted him looking our way a few times." I grabbed my snow-colada and took a long sip through the paper straw. The sweet taste of strawberry and coconut mixed with pineapple and rum hid how drunk I was beginning to get. I could see Nick suddenly go tense in his chair, sitting up straighter, both hands on the table, eyes looking somewhere behind me.

It broke my heart. He was so scared of getting caught just being himself. It was a tragic existence. Like he was a caged circus animal, trained to act in the way that appeased his captors, ignoring the way he was born to act. He looked younger to me then, the sadness subtracting years from his twenty-three.

"Don't worry," I said, "even if they get photos, it's just two guys chatting at a themed holiday party. That's it." I tried to reassure him but felt like I missed the mark. The way he half-heartedly smirked at me only verified that.

"One of those guys who happens to be the prince of Spain, and who happens to be drooling over the other guy in front of him. Yeah, that won't end up trending." Nick's sarcasm was welcome. I enjoyed a little back-and-forth teasing.

"Drooling over me?" I batted my lashes. "Here I was thinking you just wanted another serving of that pizza."

"Are you calling me out for eating five slices?"

"I'm just impressed," I said, tilting my head, smiling. "And honestly, I've never had someone make me wish I was a slice of cheese-and-pepperoni pizza before."

Nick laughed at that, the sound coming as a sweet relief. I enjoyed the sound of his laughter, even if I'd only just become acquainted with it yesterday. It didn't feel like his laugh was anything new in my life. I felt like I'd been hearing it for years and years.

"All right, so since this is just 'two guys chatting,' let's chat." Nick leaned back in his chair, but his leg moved forward, brushing against mine. The table was covered in a thick white tablecloth that rippled to the floor, making me positive the crossing of our legs was hidden.

"Let's," I said, moving my leg up and down, rubbing it on Nick's. My jeans bunched up my ankle, feeling tighter around my crotch. "So, Nick, what's your daily life like, then? As a prince?"

Loud pop music filled the room, and the tables surrounding us had been emptied as people got up to dance, drinks high in the air, so I was sure no one could overhear us.

"Should I give you the real version or the dressed-up one?"

"What kind of question is that." I arched my brow. "The real one." Nick's leg pushed against mine, pressing my legs together, adding pressure to my growing bulge.

"Well, it depends on the day and what era of my life we're talking about. When I was in my late teens, all I'd do was sleep and go out to party, with very little school on the side. Somehow, I managed to pass everything I needed to and went on to university, where I think my professors were terrified of flunking a prince, and so they let me skate on through. Those days had me drinking even more. I was definitely hiding my pain, stuffing it down with bottles. I never let anyone see, and for the most part, I don't think anyone cared. They all wanted the next story, and a drunk prince could deliver a story much better than a sober one. So I did."

"So you've never talked to anyone? About how you've felt?"

Nick shook his head, his eyes turning down at the glass of vodka cranberry in his hands. "It was pretty lonely. I almost broke and told this one girl I'd been seeing. She made me feel absolutely terrible, every single day. And not because of anything she did. I just saw her falling more and more in love by the day, and meanwhile I was drifting further away. So I almost told her what was really going on."

"What happened?"

"I broke up with her instead. Moved on to someone else

—a girl who was clearly in it just for the throne. For the money and the paparazzi and the designer jewelry. That was easy for me. Being with someone who had no real connection to me, because I knew I could never connect with them."

"You protected yourself by surrounding yourself with monsters."

"Basically. Yeah." His gaze dropped. "Except for my last girlfriend, Cristella. She was a good one, too. It broke my heart breaking hers."

I wanted to reach across the table and put my hand on his. Wanted to draw his eyes up with a kiss, one that told him he no longer had to be scared.

Of course, it was a fragile dream that shattered moments after it formed. I couldn't reach over. I couldn't kiss him. I couldn't do anything that I wanted to for fear of someone seeing. Our connection had to be hidden by a tablecloth.

"You should never have to do that again—surround yourself with empty relationships," I said, speaking with conviction.

"I don't want to."

It barely registered to me that I was consoling royalty. Nick appeared princely to me after finding out his true heritage, but still, he felt so *grounded*. Like he had grown up just down the street from me, went to the same school as me, watched the same cartoons as me.

"I can tell you aren't a monster, Shy."

My breath hitched. I swallowed a lump in my throat. Hearing Nick call me by my nickname, and the way he said it, it... fuck. It did something to me.

Or maybe it was the fact that his leg rubbed harder against mine under the table, as if the desperation between us was seconds from screeching like a boiling teakettle. "I'm not," I said.

Under the table, I kicked back my foot and slipped off my shoe, my sock pulling off with it.

I couldn't take it. Nick rubbing his leg against mine was making me wild. I wanted to show him how he could connect with me, how I could be everything he wanted and more.

Nick, who had been wearing sandals, must have kicked them off, because my bare foot rested against his, the warmth and softness of our skin on skin lighting a fire in my chest. Nick's gaze locked on mine, and his tongue traced the lines of his upper lip.

"What, uh, else does a prince do?" I asked, my wires crossing.

Nick, wearing the cockiest fucking smile ever, answered with a simple "This."

And, before I could ask what he meant, he leaned a little farther back in his chair and lifted his leg, his foot pushing my thighs apart, landing directly on my hard bulge. His smirk grew as he started to rub. My jaw parted, and I was sure I must have looked dumbfounded to anyone who was watching, but there was no way of knowing that Nicholas Silva, the prince of freaking Spain, was currently giving me a foot job, the two of us glowing under the ocean-blue lighting.

"Sounds, very, you know." I swallowed. Flames licked at my chest. "Like you do very important things."

"Very."

He rubbed a little harder. I started lifting my hips up and down, a motion that couldn't be discernible whatsoever, but a motion that built up an immense pressure in my balls. I wanted to grab my drink but was scared I would end up trembling and dropping the damn thing.

"Did you both transcend into another dimension?" The question and voice threw me out of the spell. I jerked up in my seat, planting my foot underneath me again. Nick sat up as well, leaving my boner aching under the table.

"Hey, Jada," we both said in weird unison. Who knew getting edged by a foot job would telepathically link us?

"Sorry, am I interrupting?"

Both Nick and I shook our heads. "No, no," we echoed each other again.

"Riiiight." Jada threw me a smile like she was throwing a dagger, pointed and deadly if it wasn't caught right.

I smiled back, hoping it didn't look like I was caught with my hands down my pants.

Which just so happened to be exactly where I wanted them right now.

Jada grabbed a seat next to me, her sweater jingling up a storm as she sat. The tiny silver bells that were glued down her chest spelled out "Ho, Ho, Ho." She started to look around, most likely for her boyfriend. I reached under the table and quickly pulled my sock back on, slipping my shoe on right after. Nick seemed as cool as an igloo-chilled cucumber, not giving away any hints that he had been jerking me off with his foot only seconds earlier.

Jada waved someone down from the crowd. Ace came through, Rex standing tall right behind him. Ace's sweater jingled when he sat, although much less than Jada's had. I couldn't hold back the laugh from how ridiculous his sweater was.

"What? Still gives you the giggles?" He wiggled his chest, the lone ball jingling against him.

The sweater truly won top prize in the ugly competition. It was made of a thick, scratchy-looking material with threads coming out every which way. It was a deep red in color, almost resembling a scabbed-up wound. There were small frills around the sleeves and neck, adding a subtle ugly touch that enhanced the look even more.

But the chef's kiss of it all was the embroidering on Ace's chest. It was of a cat wearing a Santa hat, but the cat happened to be walking away so that the center of Ace's chest was taken up by a furry butthole. The tail slinked upward, and the legs crisscrossed, making it appear as if the cat, with its oversized Santa hat, was disappearing into Ace's body, leaving us with a view of his ass and the dangling silver ball that hung from it, as if his business in the litter box hadn't been completely finished.

Ace gave his chest a wiggle again, the table cracking up. Rex's sweater was more subdued in its ugliness. It was an off-blue color, with oversized snowflakes stitched across the chest and arms, silver glitter sprinkled haphazardly across it.

"I just love how your sweaters match," Ace said, pointing between Nick and me. Because of course he would catch on to the similarities and call them out.

Jada looked at us, nodding as if she'd just solved a tough sudoku. "You're right. That's so funny."

Our sweaters matched because Nick hadn't brought one and I had packed two when Mason and I were still together and forgot to take them out. My sweater, a blue-

and-red creation, was terribly stitched with a smiling Santa that also might have been crying. He was lifting a beer mug to the side of the sweater, which made sense when I stood next to Nick, who had an elf on his, also stitched in the same terrible fashion, also holding a mug to the side of his sweater.

Before I could think up of a reason why our sweaters matched, I spotted someone in the crowd. He wasn't dancing or drinking, but he was looking our way intently.

It was him again. The man with the bald head and maroon tinsel sweater. That's when I saw he had his phone out and pointed toward us. I noticed something on his hand; a tattoo? A birthmark? It was hard to tell under the lights. Then I saw the barest hint of a flash go off.

It was enough for me to want a few words with the man.

"Guys, I'll be right back. Give me a few minutes."

I could feel Nick watch me as I stood and left the table. I started toward the man, who looked up from his phone screen and locked eyes with me. There was a brief moment of fear crossing his face before it went neutral again, the blues and whites of the igloo wall shining off his head. He turned and began to make his way through the crowd, toward the large exit sign above the open double doors. I sped up, accidentally shoving someone and offering a quick apology, not wanting to lose the guy.

He turned. I followed him, the exit sign shining like the North Star. But instead of going through it, the man made another turn, digging deeper into the sweater-adorned crowd, everyone laughing and chatting and dancing, none the wiser to the mini pursuit going on in their midst.

I went on tiptoes, looking over the crowd, spotting the

bald head. I went through the dance floor, cutting past the bar, my power walk bordering on a full-out run.

He threw a glance over his shoulder, his big eyes catching mine again. It made me sure that I had the right guy.

We continued walking away from the exits, deeper into the crowd. Was he trying to lose me? It was admittedly getting difficult figuring out which sweater was his. People were bumping into me, some asking to dance.

I kept walking, my eye on the bald head that would weave in and out of the crowd. But I was catching up. He was getting closer. I could almost reach out and grab him by his sweater.

And then shit hit the fan. Or, well, the *ship* hit the fan. At least, that's what it felt like when the ship suddenly rocked to one side, throwing me off my feet. This would have been fine, except I was right next to the table holding the massive Frosty the Snowman cake. When I reached out to stabilize myself, I pushed down on the table. This sent the cake flying into the air, where the head dislodged and came falling down, straight onto my head, landing on top of me with a delicious and loud splat. I couldn't see or hear anything past the vanilla cake that now covered my entire face.

I hoped people were at least getting photos, because I had a feeling I looked absolutely crazy.

11 NICHOLAS SILVA

"You looked so funny," I said, handing my phone over to Shy so he could see the photos again as he finished toweling off his head. He had already cracked up at them for a good fifteen minutes, but he just couldn't get enough it seemed, probably in the same way I couldn't get enough of his bubbly laughter.

He cracked up again. "I look nuts." He handed me back the phone. I looked at the screen, finding myself laughing along with Shy.

He really did appear crazy. There he was, standing next to a destroyed cake, wearing his ugly sweater and a pair of tight jeans, his head seemingly replaced by a frosted Frosty head, the carrot for the nose having fallen off so he was left with a hole where his real nose started poking out. One of the chocolate button eyes had also fallen, making him look even more rabid.

It was a sight to behold, and I was so fucking glad I got a photo of it.

Shiro leaned over the bathroom counter and wiped at the edges of his face with a clean wet towel I had given him. We were in my bathroom, where I figured he would want to clean up, especially after I mentioned the rainfall shower-head. His eyes (although surrounded with thick white frost-ing) lit up when I mentioned the showerhead.

He stepped back, the white lights of my bathroom glowing across his body. He had taken off his shirt, keeping on the jeans, which hung low off his cut hips. He looked at himself in the mirror, checking for any stray frosting.

"All right, I think I just need a shower to get rid of the rest of Frosty's entrails."

I snorted. "Still can't believe you murdered Frosty the Snowman tonight."

"I didn't murder him! He attacked me. It was self-defense."

"Sure. We'll see if the jury takes that. I hear the North Pole has a very rough court system."

"Yeah, I'm sure Judge Rudolph has a nose for picking up on bullshit," said Shy, his face cracking into a big grin. I spotted a dot of frosting on the corner of his lip.

"Wait, I think I see Frosty's liver."

With a chuckle, Shiro moved for the towel, but I grabbed his hand. "Here, let me take it off for you."

His gaze dropped to my lips as I went for it, kissing the side of his lip, flicking my tongue across the frosting, the sweet taste of it lingering on my tongue for a few seconds before disappearing.

"There you go," I said.

"Oh, now you've got some." It was Shiro's turn to push in for a kiss. This one wasn't on the edge of my lips. He landed directly in the center, my lips parting for him. His tongue slipped in, sliding against mine. When he pulled away, we were both smiling. "There. All better."

"Go get in the shower," I said, slapping Shiro's ass playfully. "You murderer."

Shiro gasped, putting a hand to his chest.

His very sexy and lickable chest.

"Whatever happened to innocent until proven frosty?"

"That went out the window when I witnessed the entire thing myself." I crossed my arms. "Aren't you supposed to be the detective?"

Shiro cocked his head and nodded, sucking on his teeth. "Oookay, wow. Well, maybe your eyes deceived you? Ever think of that?" Shiro spoke as he started to unbutton his jeans. He turned and walked over to the shower, pushing aside the glass door and turning it on. The ship gave another strong rock to the side, but nowhere near as bad as the one during the party.

"All right, banana boy, I'll let you shower."

"You're never going to let me forget that, are you?"

"Nope."

"Well," Shy said, "just so you know, I'm not wearing bananas today."

"No? What's on the menu today, then?"

A small fire appeared behind his golden eyes. "We've got..." He unzipped and tugged his jeans down, revealing a pair of sexy light-blue briefs, no bananas in sight unless you counted the one between his legs. His bulge was barely contained by the thin material. His cock curved downward, I could see the line of his head shadowed against the light blue. "Just some simple blue."

"Nothing about you is simple, Shy."

He tilted his head up, his gaze locked with mine, those embers growing, jumping the distance that separated us and spreading through me. I swallowed, taking him in up and down, from his sexy toes to the head of messy wet black hair. He had managed to get off most of the frosting with the towel, but a couple strands still showed white. I wanted to run my hands through it, mess it up even more.

"You're fucking beautiful."

His mouth opened, but no words came. I didn't need words. In that moment, all I needed was him. I crossed the distance between us, colliding with a kiss. I cupped his head in my hands and steered us backward, the kiss consuming my entire being. I felt the cold counter behind Shiro and pushed him against it.

Our bodies together made a kind of music that spoke to my fucking soul. And I still didn't even have him on me, not in the way I wanted.

"Take these off," I said, my lips wet. I tugged on Shiro's blue briefs which barely contained his erection.

He listened to me, stepping away from the counter and pulling his briefs down. His hard length sprung free, angled up into the air, throbbing, the pink head practically begging to be sucked, already wet with a drop of clear precome. It was the first time I'd ever seen a hard dick in person besides my own, and fuucck, all I could think was, *Why did I wait this long?*

I moved back, wanting to admire Shy in all his manly glory.

And *coño* did he look glorious. The soft white lights of the bathroom fell across his body like a glowing waterfall, highlighting the curvature of his muscles, creating small shadows that cut across his six-pack, individually defining each rippling ab. His muscular chest dipped and rose with every breath, his nipples already perked, my mouth already watering.

This was exactly what I wanted. I felt like Shy's body was the last fucking coke bottle in the desert, and I was deathly dehydrated. Never had I looked at a woman's body, as beautiful as I thought they were, and feel this sexually attracted, this hungry. I could appreciate a woman's beauty, but I wanted to devour a man's.

There was no doubt in my heart: I was gay, and I wanted Shy in all kinds of different ways.

My gaze raked over him, dropping down to his heavy cock and balls. He had a well-groomed crown of dark hair over his thick shaft, which throbbed with a need I wanted to answer. He brought his hand down, placed a thumb on his base, gripped the rest in his hand.

"Like what you see?" he asked, a cockiness in his tone that lit me on fire.

"I fucking love it."

"Then come over here and show me how much you love it."

Shiro's confidence and cocky attitude seemed to have been magnified now that he was butt-ass naked.

Suddenly, I felt a pang of nerves hit me hard in the gut. This was the first time I'd ever been with a man. The kissing and over-the-clothes fondling I had done in the past didn't count. It didn't even hold a candle up to the experience that was having Shiro's magnificent naked figure standing in front of me, his legs open wide, his thick thighs leading up to his hard cock.

"Did I break the prince of Spain?" Shiro asked again, lazily stroking himself with a devilish smirk on his handsome face. I realized then that I hadn't even moved, just continued to stare at him like I'd been hypnotized.

"Not yet," I said cheekily, snapping out of my daze. The nerves didn't go anywhere, but the excitement inside me was stronger. I crossed the bathroom, the white tile cold against the soles of my feet. I did nothing to hide the tent that had formed in my jeans as my dick throbbed to break free.

I stopped in front of Shiro, looking down and admiring how big he was.

"Grab it," he said, letting go, making space for my hand.

His skin was velvety soft. The heat from his shaft consumed me, spreading through me, burning away any apprehension I may have had.

He felt so goddamned good. I just held him there, admiring the weight of him in my hand, the girth, the length. I stroked, a slow stroke from his base to his tip. He bit his lower lip, his eyes half-lidded as I thumbed over his slit. It may have been my first time with a man, but I already had a pretty good idea of what he'd like.

I slipped my hand down, playing with his heavy balls. I imagined him unloading them down my throat. My knees almost buckled at the thought. I looked into Shiro's eyes, seeing the embers spark behind his pupils. Our lips pushed together in a kiss of epic fucking proportions. I let go of Shiro and started working on my own pants, unbuttoning and unzipping, our tongues dancing together, gliding and tasting and probing. I loved how Shiro tasted like mint and strawberries, and I loved how his lips felt against mine, and how I could feel the hint of his stubble too.

With my pants dropped and kicked off to a corner, I brought one hand back to Shiro's hard cock and the other to the nape of his neck. I pulled him harder onto me, giving his cock a squeeze as mine throbbed through my white briefs, wet through the fabric from my precome. From his neck, I moved up to his head, my fingers finding purchase in his damp hair. He moaned for me, his cock leaking so that it smeared over my palm as I ran it across his tip.

"Fuck," I said when we broke for breath. "You're soaked."

"So are you," Shiro said, slightly breathless, his cheeks pink under the light. I followed his gaze, looking down at my about-to-split briefs. Where the head of my cock pushed against the fabric, a large wet stain was spreading, turning the fabric see-through.

"Jesus, that's fucking sexy." Shiro licked his lips and slowly went down to his knees, his hands gliding down my sides as he dropped. He kept his eyes on my leaking cock while I kept mine on his, which stood hard and strong from between his legs. I wondered briefly how he'd taste, but soon my thoughts turned to dust as Shiro began to rub his face in my bulge. He looked up, smiling as he rubbed his cheek against me, and then his lips, his other cheek. Some of my clear precome made a shiny trail against his skin as I continued to soak myself through my briefs.

From my shaft, he buried his nose between my legs, his warm breath tickling the skin of my balls which were exposed from how pulled my underwear was.

His tongue flicked against me, and I almost collapsed. "Fuuuck," I said in a breath as Shiro hooked his fingers on the dark band of my briefs and began to pull them over and off.

Shiro's eyes almost bulged from his face as he took me in, my dick now free and twitching in the air. He lifted me, smiling as he traced me from bottom to top with his tongue, flicking it under the rim of my head, sending electric shocks of pleasure shooting from my nuts, making my knees tremble.

"That's so fucking good," I said, watching as Shiro opened his mouth and took me in between his lips, his warm, wet heat wrapping around me. I gasped as Shiro swallowed me deeper, looking up at me as I disappeared into his mouth. My balls tightened against me. His tongue swirled around my shaft, around the head.

"Oh God, Shy. Take my dick. That's it. All the way."

Shiro put a hand on my stomach and another on my ass. He pulled me into his mouth, my cock halfway down his throat before he had to pull off for breath. He stroked me, his saliva working as the perfect lube, making me slick from balls to tip.

"Come," I said, helping him onto his feet.

"Oh, I plan to," he said with a chuckle.

My lips turned into an O as Shiro squeezed my wet shaft, stroking it once more for good measure. I grabbed his free hand and walked him into the living room. Sunlight beamed through the balcony door, making the gold tinsel on the Christmas tree glitter. A window was cracked open, letting in a fresh ocean breeze that washed over the space. There was an old-school record player sitting on a coffee table next to the tan leather couch. A Bing Crosby record sat on the center, the album set on the side of the record player. It was a sky-blue cover with the words *Merry Christmas* across the top in a bold green, a black-and-white picture of a smiling Bing Crosby on the side. Shiro sat down on the couch, his cock still rock hard, same as mine. I put the music on, setting down the needle. "Silent Night" started to play as I turned to Shiro, my attention falling on his pulsing shaft. He held his balls and spread his legs.

"Want a taste?"

I couldn't drop to my knees faster. I took him in both my hands, once again pausing to admire how fucking hot Shy's dick was. Like... holy fuck. Even up close, hell, *especially* up close.

"*Coño*," I said, not even knowing where to start.

I licked him to start, from the base of his shaft and up to the rim of his head. I traced him up and down, tasting his salty-sweet skin against my tongue. His scent filled me, too. It was better than any cologne or perfume I'd ever smelled. Shy had a scent that intoxicated me the longer I smelled it. Like sweet cherries and vanilla and oak, a mixture that had me seeing stars.

"Suck it, Nick."

I looked up, into Shy's eyes, half-lidded and focused on me. I opened my mouth and sucked him in, tasting my first ever dick.

And instantly fucking loving it.

His precome coated my tongue as I swirled it around him, taking only the head in at first, both hands on his twitching thighs. He moaned as I took more of him in, urging me on. I was hungry for him. I stretched my jaw open, stuffing him down, swallowing as much as I could. As a first-timer, I paid extra attention to keeping my teeth out of this, bobbing up and down his shaft with my lips wrapped around him, in tune with how he writhed on the couch, the leather squeaking against his bare skin.

I not only found myself loving how Shy tasted, but also how he was reacting. His grunts and moans sent me to fucking space, and then when his hand landed on the back of my head, it was game over. He pushed me down on his cock as he began to thrust up, fucking my throat.

It was the hottest thing to have ever fucking happened to me. I let him use my throat as he started to fuck into my face. When I gagged, he let up for a moment so I could catch my breath, and then I went right back down on his cock, going as far as I could before I had to come up again.

And again.

And again.

I started to jerk myself off. Shiro continued to fuck my face, the sounds of my balls slapping against me and his balls slapping against my chin driving me absolutely wild. Saliva dripped down onto the floor. His grunts gained an animalistic edge to them, matching the instincts roaring inside me.

"I'm going to come, Nick. You're gonna make me come."

He warned me, but I didn't pull off. I just sucked him farther into my mouth.

The first jet of come shocked me. It hit the back of my throat with a force that almost hurt. The one that followed hit just as deep, but I was ready, swallowing it down, taking him like a shot.

I had tasted myself before. It was only enough to coat my thumb when I had tried it, but Shy fed me a mouthful. It was thick and salty and intoxicating.

Shiro twitched and spasmed as he lifted his legs, squeezing his thighs around my head as he exploded down my throat.

I couldn't take it. I came with him, blowing my load onto the floor. Thick splats sounded as I came in an endless stream, still tasting Shy in my mouth even as I pulled off, shouting with the sound of my climax, come dripping off my lip.

When it was all said and done, the two of us were fucking spent. I looked up and wiped my mouth, smiles cracking across both of our flushed faces. I collapsed forward, my face falling on Shiro's hard abs, his softening cock pressed against my chest, making me sticky and wet.

"That was... wow. I'm fucking speechless," I said, out of breath.

Shiro's fingers traced gentle circles across my shoulders, slipping me into a trance.

"And that was your first time? With a man?"

"First blow job." I smiled against his abs. "How'd I do?"

"I don't know. I might have to do some detective work. I don't believe that was your first time, Prince Nick."

I playfully nipped at his skin. "Just Nick." I kissed the same spot I bit. "And it was my first time. Glad I impressed... banana boy."

We stayed in my room for hours after, playing around, exploring each other, kissing and stroking and sucking. It was bliss. If Shiro didn't have to get back down to his friends, I don't think I ever would have left the room. I didn't care where the cruise ship took us next—all I wanted was Shy's naked body against mine.

I especially didn't want to leave the room when it meant going back out there and having to play pretend all over again. Having to keep some distance between me and the man of my wet dreams all because I was scared someone would take an unsolicited shot of us.

But we had to do it. Reality trumped the scorching fantasy that had played out behind closed doors.

At least, for now it did.

12 SHIRO BROOKS

FOUR DAYS LATER

The cruise ship glowed underneath the lights that shined on it from shore. There were red, green, and white rows of light that emitted from each level of the ship, sometimes blinking and sometimes steady, adding a magical touch. The sleek, modern design of the ship, with its seventeen decks and mostly glass exterior, made it seem as if it were something from the future, having traveled time and landed on the shores of St. John's Island, where Nick and I walked, heading toward a popular market, live music and the sound of cheerful crowds drifting toward us.

We laughed over Nick's childhood fear of the movie *Jumanji* and how he was scared a stampede would burst through his home library at any second.

"The fact that you even have a home library is still crazy to me," I said. "Which, duh, you grew up in a palace." It would hit me out of nowhere. How I was hanging out and quickly falling for the prince of freaking Spain.

And yes. I was falling. Really damn hard.

This "fake" friendship turned real had exploded as quickly as a wildfire driven by strong, hot winds. Like a hurricane on fire. Over the past few days, I had found more in common between me and Nick than I felt like I ever had between me and Mason. And this was even taking into consideration the fact that Nicholas was a certified prince next in line for the throne. As opposite as you could get from my life as an immigrant and my career as a detective. The only throne that had been waiting for me was the driver's seat with the scratched-up black leather inside the beat-up and sunburnt Honda Civic my dad had given me for my eighteenth birthday.

And still, I felt completely comfortable around Nick, and I loved spending every single second I could around him. It helped that he got along really well with my friends, too. We even came clean about Nick's real name, although we held back his last name when Ace asked randomly.

So a lot of the time it was all of us hanging out and exploring. But when it was just me and Nick ... that was when the fireworks went off at a constant rate.

And trust me, I tried to find as much time as I could to just make it me and Nick. It helped that I had been sleeping over in his penthouse suite every night, where we'd stay up for way too long, either playing with each other or just talking, naked, lying on top of the covers and eating room service brought up by a butler.

I was excited about today's excursion, especially since it was another day of just Nick and me. It was Christmas Eve, and the cheer of the season practically sparkled in the air. We walked into the market together. It was a perfectly romantic setup and one I wanted to stroll through hand in hand with Nick.

Not that we were even anything official, where I could expect hand-holding status. And yet all I wanted to do was reach out and grab him by the hand as we walked past the arch of lights marking the entrance to the market, two Christmas palm trees bordering either side of it.

I couldn't, though. I had to keep acting as if we were simply friends, hanging out on a cruise together.

You know, just two cruising bros, cruising the seas together, broing it out.

Two bros, jerking each other off and licking the come off each other's abs.

Just bro stuff.

It didn't help that I still hadn't made much progress on who the stowaway paparazzo was. I found it interesting that none of the photos of me covered in cake and Nick helping me had made it to the tabloids. It made me think that maybe the man, who I seemed to have scared away, just wasn't around to take the photos. I hadn't seen him anywhere since the incident at the ugly-sweater party. I had made sure to keep an eagle eye out for him everywhere we went but didn't spot him anywhere. I even did a couple of laps around the entire ship, which took me hours, with the sole purpose of finding him, but he had somehow remained out of sight. When we stopped at Grand Cayman for two days, I wondered if maybe he had gotten off, decided to just fly home from the island. Maybe he felt like his gig was up and he'd rather spend his holidays with family instead of stalking the prince. It was a long shot and one I highly doubted, but until I spotted him again, I had to think of possible alternatives.

There was also the chance that this man had nothing to do with the leaked photos. Maybe I needed to be looking closer. At someone who had full access to Nick, and worked as a shadow alongside him.

Luna. I felt like Nick genuinely trusted her, but that didn't mean she was off my list. As a detective, I had to follow my own instincts, not anyone else's. I learned that very quickly after my first few cases at Stonewall. It's why I had spent about half an hour asking her questions out on the deck, and she had answered all of them just fine.

"And you're sure no one followed you from the palace?" I remembered asking her, noticing that her eyes barely ever left Nick, who had sat by the bar and was chatting with Ace and Rex.

"There's always a small possibility, but, honestly, I don't think any paparazzo is that determined or skilled."

"Have you noticed anyone on the ship who might have recognized Nick?"

She thought on that one. "No, Nick's surprisingly been able to keep a low profile. Even with his infatuation with you."

"Infatu... me... you think, I mean, you've noticed?"

"It's my job to notice every little thing that goes on around Nick." She had given me a playful wink. "It'll be my secret of course."

The talk soon got derailed. After meeting her, I came away understanding why Nick trusted her.

The paparazzo's identity remained a mystery.

For now, though, it was just me and Nick (and Luna somewhere off in the distance), currently walking through the bright and festive outdoor market on St. John's Island, celebrating with a Christmas festival that took over the entire island. The crowd wasn't very dense, so I could easily tell that no one was paying any extra attention to us. It was the evening, so the sun was midway down the horizon, the sky painted in bold purples and warm pinks. There were Christmas lights strung up everywhere you looked, wrapping up the lengths of the palm trees, hanging off the market stalls and creating a blast of holiday light everywhere you looked.

"Check this out," Nick said, motioning over to a large stall selling an assortment of necklaces, all different colors and styles laid out on open shelves, on top of red pillows. "I think one of these would look good on you." He picked up a beaded necklace made from black-and-white beads, glittering like little gemstones. He held against my neck. The merchant smiled and agreed with Nick, saying it would look great with a matching pair.

"You think so?" Nick asked.

"Oh yes." She grabbed a green-and-white necklace from the display and held it up to Nick. "No, hold on." She set that one back down and grabbed a navy blue and white necklace. She held that one and looked between me and Nick.

"Now you two look like good boyfriends."

My face almost cracked in surprise, but I somehow

managed to keep my expression neutral. Nick's cheeks turned a rosy red, which I actually found quite fucking adorable. He stumbled on his words before saying, "We'll take them."

She rolled up our necklaces as she hummed a happy tune. We walked away from the stall with the two necklaces, leaving her with a hundred dollars, eighty of that being left as a gift by Nick. She had nearly been brought to tears by the generous gift, shouting gratefully to us as we left, "Merry Christmas!"

"That was really kind of you," I said, admiring the necklaces before I turned my gaze to Nick so I could admire the prince at my side. Even though the sun was almost gone, he still wore a cap low on his head. I could still make out his eyes, though, like two lighthouses I had memorized the route to over the past few days. I could always find his eyes.

"The necklaces were just *that* good."

"Mhmm."

I could tell he was bullshitting. He looked at me with a twinkle underneath the shadow of his cap. He hadn't given her that money because of the necklaces. He'd given it to her because he wanted to.

"Well, I'm sure she's going to have a great Christmas."

"How were your holidays? As a kid?"

I wasn't surprised by the question. Nick had asked me a ton of questions over the past couple of days, and I'd done the same with him. Our curiosity for each other was endless. Like Newton searching for the laws of gravity.

"They were great. I loved Christmas. My parents would do the whole 'cookies and carrot' thing the night before, and I freaking loved waking up to an empty plate and an empty glass of milk. Don't get me wrong, the gifts were great, too, but something about the cookies, milk, and carrot being gone made everything magical. I loved it. Every year. Then after I found my gifts stuffed inside my mom's closet one holiday and realized Santa wasn't real, I still left out the plate of treats. And still, they disappeared. By the time I was a teen, we joked that I was just aiding in my dad's weight problem, but they still ate the cookies and carrot and drank the milk."

Nick, smiling, narrowed his eyes. "Carrot?"

"That's what you got from the story?"

"No, of course not."

I laughed, playfully slapping Nick's chest, catching myself too late. I momentarily freaked and scanned the crowd, but no one seemed to be paying any attention to us.

"The carrot was for the reindeer," I said.

"One carrot for all twelve reindeer? Wow. I'm calling PETA."

I chuckled at that. "And how about you? Anything I could call PETA about?"

"Absolutely not." Nick held his chin. "I left a trough of organically sourced meal for all twelve of the reindeer along with a five-star course for Santa and a separate buffet for the elves."

"Of course you would," I said, laughing, taking in the cool ocean breeze, feeling like I was on top of the world. I wore a pair of khaki shorts and a light-gray button-down shirt, short-sleeved. Normally, my parents rented out a cabin in Tennessee and had us spend Christmas there, so I was used to being bundled up and sitting by a crackling fire. But this variation of the holidays felt equally enchanting.

"The holidays were a fun time," Nick said as we continued our leisurely stroll, walking past a stand of colorful soap bars and balls that smelled great. "The palace is always decked out, and there are a lot of fun events through the month. It does get tiring by the end of it, though. Especially lately. It's why I knew I had to get out of there this Christmas. I couldn't sit around a table, having dinner with my parents and the prime minister, acting like everything was completely fine and dandy. The idea made my skin crawl."

"I take it you aren't regretting your choice?"

"Not in the slightest," Nick said, shooting me a smile that lit up my entire world, from north to south pole. "How about you? Are you regretting our fake-friendship agreement?"

"Oh yeah, duh. I hate this." I motioned him up and down. "Hanging out with you? It's literally the worst thing under the sun. Next to having sex with Chris Evans or winning a gajillion dollars."

"Those all sound like wonderful things."

I cocked a brow. "Huh. They do, don't they?"

Nick laughed and I drank in the sound.

"I definitely don't regret it," I said, being more serious. "I was nervous about coming on this trip. I thought I'd be an awkward seventh wheel, always being reminded that my relationship crashed and burned. I thought I'd be miserable. But I haven't. I've been having the best time of my life, and I don't miss my ex at all. I feel like I've found peace in the breakup. It's a really great Christmas gift."

"Good, I'm glad you've found your peace. I'm slowly but surely finding my own."

He did something then that surprised the gay glittering crap out of me. He put an arm around me, not even around my shoulder but around my waist, and he pulled me into his side. He gave me a quick but searing kiss on the side of my head before letting me go.

It felt like a magnitude eight earthquake had finished rocking through me. I half expected to blink and then reopen my eyes to a devastated market, everyone knocked to their feet by the force of the emotion that exploded inside me.

We both continued walking through the market nonchalantly, as if something didn't shift between us, something with the power of two tectonic plates tearing the world apart.

"Oh, check out these books," Nick said, drifting over to a book stall. I followed him in, making a futile attempt to look at the books and not at the handsome prince who had swept me off my feet. As I was trying not to stare at Nick, I spotted someone else across the way. A bald man wearing a red shirt and standing against a tall brick wall, his attention turned toward us before flicking away. He held a phone in his hand and appeared to be hurrying away.

"Nick, wait here," I said, deciding I wasn't going to lose this guy again. I wanted to ask him a few questions, and I was determined to do just that.

13 NICHOLAS SILVA

I thumbed through a bin of old books, checking out the stained spines, reading the different titles but not registering any of them. All I could really think about was the kiss I had planted on Shy's head. A moment when "fuck it" energy had overtaken me. I had been overwhelmed with how good I felt, walking through the market with Shy by my side. It had felt so fucking right, I had to express it. I couldn't keep the happiness to myself, and so I shared it with a spontaneous kiss.

I hadn't even scanned the crowd for any cameras or prying eyes. It had been that strong of a push. Would I regret it? Maybe in the future, but right then and there, I didn't. As I mindlessly looked through the books, I found myself smiling.

It had been a common occurrence now that I'd been

hanging out with Shy. I'd wake up with a smile, something that never happened to me before. I hated the mornings and never thought I'd be one of those people who woke up with birds chirping by their heads and a smile that looked as if they'd found a glittering pot of gold.

Maybe it was because I felt like I'd been waking up next to my own personal pot of gold. Shiro had been sleeping over, and every morning, I'd find his warm back pressed against my chest, our bodies curled together, our legs entwined. It was a feeling I couldn't quite describe. One I'd been searching for my entire life.

Who would have thought that I would have felt more at home, floating through the Atlantic Ocean, with Shiro in my arms than I would have felt with any of my ex-girl-friends back at the palace?

I looked over to Shiro, wanting to admire him some more. I loved watching him, both from close and from afar. I liked memorizing the way he walked, with his hands relaxed and his butt perked out. He had a bubble butt I loved to play with. It had quickly become a favorite pastime of mine. I loved giving him a slap and watching it jiggle, or rubbing myself against him, feeling those globes of muscle press onto me. I had wanted to get between those cheeks and feel myself sinking into him on multiple occasions, but I held back each time.

"No, you listen to me."

The angry words came from the man Shiro was talking to. I instantly went on guard, sensing the tension that rolled off the pair. I could almost see the anger in the man's face, radiating off his bald head like heat off a strip of sun-battered pavement.

I moved closer to them. I didn't recognize the man, but it seemed like Shiro did. Was he the one taking our photos? Had Shy solved it?

"I just wanted to ask a few questions, that's all," Shiro said, his hands up in an attempt to defuse the situation.

"For what? Are you accusing me of something? Fuck that, I'm just having a good time on my vacation. I already showed you my phone. Fuck you."

The man stepped forward, getting into Shy's face.

"What's going on here?" I asked, walking into the lion's den.

"Don't worry about it," Shy said, putting a hand out between me and the red cherry of a man. It didn't help that his bloodred shirt matched the shade that was consuming his entire face. "I was just leaving."

"Oh, so now you want to leave? Who's this? Your partner? You two cops?"

Getting this close allowed me to smell the alcohol fumes wafting from between the man's chapped lips. He was ten times too trashed. I looked around, wondering if anyone could claim this buffoon.

"All right, forget it. You can't even send a text, much less a paparazzi photo." Shiro turned, nudging me with his shoulder. "Let's go."

Shiro had made a terrible mistake. By turning his back on the drunk asshole, he gave the man an opening. I saw it happening in slow motion. The man reached out with his grubby hands and grabbed Shy's collar, bunching it up in his fist. He pulled him backward and had another fist ready to crush into Shy's lower back. I burst into action, lurching forward to grab at the man's arm. Shouts erupted around us.

The man's punch never landed. As Shiro got pulled back, he did something pretty extraordinary. He used the momentum to jump upward, using a solid brick wall as purchase for his feet. He seemed like Spider-Man, climbing up the wall and jumping over the drunk man, landing gracefully behind him. He grabbed the man in a headlock, the dude's eyes bulging out of his skull from the shock mixed with the alcohol. He must not have known which way was up.

"Whoa, whoa!" It was Luna, my protective shadow. She had come running, her colorful floral button-up lifted over her concealed weapon, her hands on the gun, ready to take it out. "What's going on here?"

"We were just leaving," Shiro said, throwing the man down onto the ground. He stayed there as we walked away, heading through the market, which now had every eye turned toward us, Luna close behind us.

"What the hell happened?" I asked as we exited the market, walking toward the lit-up ship. "Who was that?"

"Sorry, I thought he was the one who'd been taking the photos. I've spotted him around... at least I'm pretty sure I have. And I thought I saw his flash go off. I went over to ask him where he was from and why he was so interested in us. I didn't expect him to go from one to a hundred out of nowhere."

"He was trashed. He's probably been looking for a fight, and you gave it to him."

I looked over my shoulder, checking to make sure we'd left the guy in the market. I saw Luna walking behind us, her shirt hiding the gun. She was watching us but talking to someone next to her. I realize then it was her mom, whose pencil-thin eyebrows were scrunched together in worry. She threw a glance at me and subtly waved. I had a feeling she wasn't sure who knew what, so she kept her recognition of me to herself. I shot a smile back before turning my attention back to Shy.

"Do you think it was him?" I asked. The steel panels of the dock trembled underneath us as we approached the ship.

"I asked to see his phone. That's what got him the most pissed. But he had shown it to me just before you walked over. None of the photos were of us. Plus, I remember seeing a birthmark on the man I was originally suspect of, back at the sweater party, but this guy's hands didn't have anything." Shiro's head dropped. "I don't think we've found the leaker."

"That's okay. We'll keep looking." I clapped my hands, not wanting this to destroy the mood. "In the meantime, let's just have a good time. What's on the agenda for tonight?"

"Tonight?" He shrugged, a grin spreading across his face. As we walked into the atrium, the lights from the chandelier caught Shy's eyes, making them glitter like gems. "Well, there's the blizzard foam party happening in a couple of hours. I think Ace and Rex really wanted us to go with them."

"Let's do it, then," I said, having never been to a foam party before.

"Perfect." We stopped at the glass elevator. "So, about that aerial stunt move you pulled back there. I didn't know I was dating James Bond."

The word slipped out of my mouth as easy as Shiro

twirled over that man. I couldn't take it back either. What was said was said. I looked into his eyes, feeling like I had just stuffed an entire sock into my mouth.

"I'm into parkour," Shy answered, a mischievous grin playing across his face. "And I'm into dating you, too. By the way."

"Good," I said, trying to play it off as if I meant to say it in the first place. In truth, I wasn't sure of what the situation between us really was. We had started off as a fiery kiss inside of a bookshop to then fall into a fake friendship which exploded into a real relationship in a matter of days. Did I think we were exclusively dating? No, of course not. Did I know I wanted to hang out with Shiro and Shiro only? Hell to the fuck yes I did. I loved falling asleep next to him and waking up next to him, and I loved everything else that happened in between. There was still more to discover about each other, that part was also clear, but wasn't that the whole point of dating someone? I wanted to have that time of discovery, where I found all the gems inside his soul, even the ones that were cracked for whatever reason.

The elevator opened. We got in and rode it up to the penthouse level, where we entered my suite, and we didn't waste a single second in getting undressed and sealing this whole "dating" thing together.

WE SHOWED up at the foam party wearing only our swim trunks. Shiro looked so good in his, a pair of small green trunks that showed off the curve of his ass, making him look like he had stuffed the shorts with two basketballs.

My sky-blue trunks fit tight around my crotch, which I didn't so much mind for tonight. I enjoyed the way Shy went slack-jawed when he saw me in them.

At the door of the foam party, we got carded and were then handed our choice of a Santa hat or fluffy reindeer antlers. I went for the hat, and Shiro grabbed the antlers. He put them on, looking so fucking adorable as he half shimmied, half twerked his way into the party, music already thumping in the air.

The blizzard party was staying true to its theme. Before we entered the foam pit, we had to walk through a dimly lit hall, made to appear like the inside of a cozy cabin. There were windows painted on the walls, and each window we passed progressively grew snowier and snowier, until the final window we passed was completely covered with snow. A door stopped our path, a sign above it reading "Have a Foamy Christmas!" The music pounded on the other side of the door. We looked at each other, smiling, ready to dive in. And, in another moment of "fuck it," I leaned in and stole a quick kiss from him.

It only lasted seconds, but *fuck* was it exhilarating. Kissing another man. Kissing Shy. It thrilled me to no end. I wanted to do it for longer, but I didn't want to press my luck. Anyone could open that door and see us locking lips.

"Let's get foamy," Shy said as he opened the door, the music hitting us first. Cardi B blasted through the speakers, vibrating through my bones. The ballroom was huge, and it was covered in fluffy white foam, reaching up to my chest as we walked into it, the both of us smiling like two kids in their first candy shop. The room was packed, with bodies grinding and bumping underneath the foam, accompanying heads wearing their Santa hats and antlers smiling in drunken glee. Laser lights of all different colors shot through the room, hitting the multiple disco snowflakes and being reflected into a hundred other directions. It felt like a high-end nightclub in Madrid.

"Damn, this is crazy," Shiro said, leaning in so I could hear him over the music. "Let's get into the foam!"

He grabbed my hand for a flash of a moment before letting it go. It was dark and I didn't think anyone could even see our faces, much less take photos. I reached for Shiro's hand, grabbing it, his eyes registering surprise before they crinkled at the corners because of his smile. We walked into the foam, cool against my bare chest. It felt like we were walking into a thick fog. It smelled slightly of pine and clean linens, the scent made stronger when Shiro playfully "splashed" some of the foam in my direction, a clump of it sticking to my chin.

"It's Santa! Holy shit, and your name is Nick." Shiro covered his mouth with a hand. "Illuminati confirmed."

I laughed and pulled him in, feeling even more assured by the fact that foam now concealed us from chest down. People danced around us, moving to a throwback song, no one paying us any mind.

"So then what do you want for Christmas, Shy?"

"Hmm... aren't I supposed to be sitting in your lap for this?"

"Ho, ho, *hoooo*." I reached down and grabbed his legs before lifting him up. He let out a surprised squeak, instinctively wrapping his legs around my waist. Even though we had spent the last hour hooking up, I still had a difficult time keeping my hands off him. "This better?"

"Much," Shy said, his arms holding me around my chest, underneath the foam. To anyone on the outside, they'd just see two friends talking close so they could be heard over the music, completely unaware that those two friends had their growing dicks pressing together.

"Let's see, I want a pony, but I can settle for something I can ride like one."

"I'll see what I can do," I said, playfully reaching around and letting my fingers rub down the center of his ass, over his trunks. "Anything else?"

"Well... I guess, I wouldn't mind finding a handsome prince under the tree."

"A handsome prince, huh? I think I can manage that one, too."

"Oh, and since we're on the subject, make that hand-some prince from Spain, and have him hung like a bull."

"I can definitely deliver that." I pulled him a little closer, our bodies moving to the rhythm of the music. I barely even realized we were dancing together, Shy grinding on me as I moved us left and right. I wanted to lean in and kiss him, but I felt that would be too risky.

Under the foam, Shy put a hand on my chest. He leaned in dangerously close. I could feel his breath against my lips. "Before we get too carried away, let's find Ace and Rex." He dropped his feet to the ground.

We made our way through the foam, keeping our eyes peeled for the innocent-faced Ace and his burly boyfriend. We spotted Jada and Ken, but they were busy tongue wrestling against the wall, and we didn't want to interrupt. It wasn't much longer until we bumped into Ace and Rex, grinding up on each other like they were trying to start a fire for everyone to gather around.

"Oh hey, studmuffins," Ace said, bouncing off of Rex to give us each a foam-covered hug.

"Hey, guys." Rex hugged us, too.

"We were actually gonna go get drinks, come with!" Ace motioned over to the side of the room where the foam seemed to end. There was a bar set against the wall, where a tall and full Christmas tree sat, its branches flocked with fake snow, its top glowing with a bright golden star.

At the bar, we took stock of how wet the foam had made us. It looked like the four of us had taken a dip in the pool. I ordered myself a Moscow mule and got Shy a vodka tonic. We cheered when Ace and Rex got their drinks, an excitement buzzing in the air, heightened by the great music and the better drinks.

Ace leaned on Rex as we stood by a tall round table. "I invited Lou," he said, "but he's going to the outdoor movie by the pool, and then he's breaking up with his girlfriend."

Shiro almost spit out his drink. "He's breaking up with her?"

"No, just joking. Well, less of a joke and more of me speaking my wants to the universe. I don't know. Some girl in the suite next to us is really into horoscopes and crystals, and she told me I had to do that more often. Speak things into existence." He lifted up his swirling red and pink drink. "So, here's to that."

The group laughed at that.

"Well, Lou could definitely find better," Shy said. "She's barely said more than five sentences the entire time we've been here. I think she's trying to assimilate with her phone."

"That's a very strong possibility," Ace said. After hanging out with them for the past week, I had come to learn that Shy and Ace were the closest in the group. They seemed to have shared the most, and their experiences definitely shaped them into being close friends.

"What have you guys been up to today?" Rex asked, his booming voice not having a difficult time to be heard over the music.

Before I could answer, something had caught Shy's attention. He nudged me with an elbow and tilted his head back, pointing his chin.

I looked to where Shiro pointed. Luna walked toward us, having taken the route around all the foam, staying completely dry in her jeans and shirt. She held something in her hand, and there was an urgent look in her eyes. I'd seen it only a few times before. Once when there had been a credible terrorist threat on the palace and another when Eli had been found unconscious in the garden after eating something he shouldn't have. Thankfully, both of those situations had good outcomes, but I'd never forgotten Luna's face, one that appeared twisted in pain and set in stone at the same time.

What could have...

Another photo.

14 SHIRO BROOKS

Nick had walked away with Luna, who appeared as if she was acting as the bearer of some very bad news. I half expected her to pull out a scythe and say she was now the grim reaper and our time was up. Instead, she took Nick to the side of the room and showed him something on his phone. I tried not to pay too much attention to Nick and instead tried to listen to the story Ace was animatedly telling, but I couldn't help myself, especially when Nick's face lost all color and his jaw dropped, covered by a hand which quickly turned into an angry fist. Without even looking back, Nick stormed off, leaving Luna in his wake, trailing behind him with a jogger's pace.

"What? What happened?" Ace started to look around, trying to figure out what had caught my attention.

Should I chase after Nick? Part of me wanted to, but I

didn't move from my spot. I just shook my head, as confused as Ace.

"Where'd your boyfriend run off to?"

The question almost knocked me off my feet. The way Ace had asked it sounded as if there was no arguing that Nick's proper title was "boyfriend."

"He, um, he's not—we're not... I—"

"Shy, come clean. You two are together. I can practically smell his dick on your breath."

I shouldn't have been surprised by Ace coming out with an X-rated phrase, but here I was, guffawing in shock.

"What? Is it someone else's dick I'm smelling?"

Rex laughed behind him. "Leave him alone. Look how red you're making him."

"He's getting red because he knows it's true!"

"It's not true," I said, feebly trying to keep up appearances even though my skin felt like it had caught fire. "We've just become good friends. That's all."

"Yeah, good friends. And me and Rex are two nuns practicing for the big nun exam."

"A big... you're crazy." I hoped I could get off this topic.

"And you're hiding something." Ace wasn't going to let it go.

"I'm not hiding anything." But I was still going to try.

"Then text Mason right now. Tell him you miss him."

Annnd, I was done trying. "Fine. Fine. It's true. You're right, Nick and I have been together. Kind of. It's complicated, all right? But Mason's no longer in the picture. We're done. We've been done for a month and some weeks now."

"Yeah, I had a feeling about that. Especially since I had talked to him a few weeks ago and he already told me."

"What!" My head bobbed forward. "Are you serious? You knew?"

"Yup. I just wasn't going to say anything. I figured you would tell me when the time was right."

I rubbed my forehead, taken by total surprise. He hadn't given any indication he knew. Ace had always been good at keeping secrets, but kudos on him for not breaking with this one.

"And, *booooy*, can I just say one word: upgrade! You seriously went up a thousand levels with Nick, compared to Mason, for sure. I mean, Mason and me were kind of good friends in college, but with the few things you'd shared with me about you two, I knew you deserved much more. And Nick looks like much more times some."

My smile grew uncontained. "He's a good guy. A really good guy."

"So why aren't you chasing after him right now? Something bothered him. Go and soothe him." Ace purred the last of his words, rubbing up on Rex and batting his long lashes at me.

"Here," I said, handing Ace my drink. "Finish this for me. I'm going to go find my prince."

"Oooh, already calling him a prince? Damn. He really must have dicked you down good," Ace said, drinking out of both his drink and mine, the two straws in between his smiling lips.

I figured I would break the whole "prince of Spain" thing to them a little later. I laughed and waved him off, saying bye to the pair before turning around and scanning the crowd, not spotting Nick or Luna anywhere. I didn't think he would go back into the foam, and Luna definitely didn't look dressed to party in a field of foam, so I wondered if they had left the room altogether.

Outside of the party, the atmosphere was much quieter. My ears rang as I stepped out into the quiet hallway. There were a couple people walking over wearing their bikinis and swimsuits, ready to party. I went past them, heading down the hall, looking around for any sign of Nick or Luna.

I was passing a lounge area when I spotted him.

Nick stood against the green-and-red wall, his head in his hands. He looked so broken. Defeated. It crushed me. I went over to him and put a hand on his shoulder. He looked up, his eyes registering mine, his pulse matching mine, and then he shook my hand off. It felt like a slap. I didn't know what to say, where to go, what to think.

Nick walked around me, shaking his head, his hands turned to fists. "I knew it would happen. I was stupid. Stupid to think it didn't matter."

"What happened, Nick? Talk to me."

"Better yet, here. Let me show you." He held his phone out. I already knew what I was going to see, but I grabbed it anyway.

There we were, pictured walking through the Christmas market. Nick had his arm around me and his lips pressed to the top of my head. A smile of pure joy was beaming on my face. Holiday lights twinkled in the background, a pile of wreaths just next to us. The thing looked like a Hallmark card. It was actually a beautiful shot, and one I would have been proud of under different circumstances.

Instead of pride, my gut twisted in fear and dread.

There was no denying this was the prince. And there was no denying he was kissing me.

"The photo hasn't been sold yet or leaked. That's the only saving grace in this fucking disaster."

I tried not to take it personally. That he would use "disaster" when all I saw was "joy" in that photo. "Wait, then how did you get this?"

"Luna. Someone had sent it to her by accident, apparently. It just said 'here's the photo for tomorrow's edition. I want payment doubled.' Luna didn't recognize the number, and when we called back, it goes straight to a generic voicemail."

"Shit... But this could be it. Maybe this is how we find the person, then. They had to have Luna's number if they sent it to her by accident. I can talk to someone who helps out at Stonewall. Her name is Anya; she's an excellent hacker. She can figure—"

"Don't you get it? It doesn't fucking matter anymore. None of it does."

"What? But we can stop it."

"And then what? It's like a bucket riddled with bullet holes. You plug one leak and another one follows. Unless I throw the bucket away completely. Go back to hiding. Go back to hating every day of my fucking life." Nick turned to me. His eyes were glowing, but not with the light I had fallen for. It was an angry glow, made more so by the stern set of his brow, wrinkles appearing on his forehead from the tension rising in his body.

"You know what it felt like, waking up every day, knowing I had to put on my mask so that I wouldn't upset my parents? So that I don't upset the country? It felt like I woke up on a bed of glass. Every. Single. Fucking. Day." His cheeks were growing red underneath his five-o'clock shadow. "And do you know what it felt like waking up next to you? Like paradise. It didn't even matter if we were waking up in my room or on hammocks somewhere on the beach. As long as I could look to my side and see you, things felt right. No glass."

He turned from me again. His chest and back were getting red, too. The emotion inside him was rising to a breaking point.

"We can buy some time, Nick. I'll find the leaker, and that'll buy you time to figure things out."

"I have figured things out! That's the thing, Shy. I know what I want. I'm just too fucking scared to get it."

Words got caught in my throat. With his voice raised, Nick's demeanor shifted. I didn't want to say the wrong thing, but I also didn't want to say anything at all. "You can overcome that fear. You can push past it."

"I thought I could. I really did. That's why I broke up with Cristella. That's why I kissed you, why I followed you and handed you a ChapStick that wasn't even yours. I have moments of strength. But, at the end of the day, I'm a coward. One ruled not by crown but by fear. I'm scared of a fucking photo. How pathetic is that?"

He had his back to me, but the way his voice cracked made it feel like he had dug a stake through my heart. He raised his hand and wiped at his face before turning back to face me.

"That morning, the day I broke up with her... fuck. I haven't told anyone about this. I haven't even said it out loud, not to myself."

Nick's face cracked, and his lips shook before he covered them, turning away from me. It felt like I was helplessly watching from the shore as a tsunami crested on the horizon. Frozen in place and wrought with fear, I couldn't say or do anything. I wanted to reach for his hand and pull him out of the dark, cold waters he was struggling not to drown under. Instead, I wrung my hands together, my head spinning.

He gathered his strength and said, "I almost jumped."

Those three words hit me like a semitruck slamming into a sedan.

"I walked to the highest point," he continued, his voice cracking, reflecting the same cracks I felt over my heart. "I walked up there. It was early; the sun hadn't come up. No one was around. I remember a single bird, don't know what type, but it chirped and landed right on top of a lamppost. I remember everything else being covered in silence. And I said to myself, 'This is—'" His voice lilted, taking on a higher pitch. I didn't hold myself back this time. I reached out. I grabbed his hands in mine, held his gaze. I let him know I was here with him, that I was listening and absorbing his every word. My lip quivered, but I held strong for him, wanting to serve as his anchor.

He didn't take his hands from mine. He straightened his back and sniffed a few times. "I said, 'This is it.' I didn't want to keep living a lie. I knew I couldn't. Every day had been a new torture. And I didn't see a way out of it, I just didn't." He shook his head, taking a hand from mine only to wipe at his cheek. "And then something happened. Something clicked. I was looking down at the dark water, about twenty meters below me, and I realized that, as badly as I didn't want to live a lie, I also didn't want to end on the lie. I didn't want to die and not give myself a chance at something better. I'd be robbing myself. And I would have robbed everyone around me. It was like an 'aha' moment, just like the ones on TV, except this one ended up saving my life. I realized I was making a huge mistake. I stepped back, away from the banister. The bird flew away when I did, singing a song. I'd never heard a bird sing so early in the morning.

"Nick..." I had trouble speaking past my heartache. "I'm so sorry. I feel... fuck. I'm sorry. You should never have to feel like that. I never want you feeling like that. You're such a bright soul, and I mean that, Nick. You really did light up my life in a matter of days. I can't imagine how dark the world would get without you in it. Thank you for being strong."

He mustered a smile. There was a shining trail that went down his other cheek, catching the light. He rubbed at it with the back of his hand before returning it to mine. "It was hard, I can't lie. But I'm so happy I walked away that morning. Meeting you confirmed it for me. It was the exact right choice. Just like following after you was the right choice. Kissing you was the right choice."

I looked into Nick's deep blue eyes, sensing the pain that was in them floating away, like flotsam being dragged out by the tide.

"If you ever feel like you're back in that headspace, talk to me, okay?" I wanted to make sure Nick knew he'd never be alone. "No matter where you are or what time it is, call me."

"Thank you, Shy. I don't see myself slipping backward, but I do really appreciate it." He moved a little closer to me.

This had gotten so intense, I barely realized how close we were standing.

"Okay, good," I said. "I'll always be here for you."

"And I'll need is your support, especially when I come out to the world."

"You're going to come out? Nick, you'd change so many lives if you do."

He nodded, his smile stronger than before, the glint in his eyes beginning to return.

"I don't know exactly when or how, but I know now that it's what I've got to do. I don't want anyone thinking the same thoughts I did that morning at Hightower. And I think I can do that by coming out, showing kids that being out and proud is possible, even if you happen to be next in line for the throne... I've just got to tell my parents first. I think they deserve to hear it directly from me."

"I agree." I chewed the inside of my cheek. "How do you think they'll take it?"

"Honestly? No idea. It can go both ways. But I can't keep hiding it from them, especially not when I plan on kissing you nonstop."

"Nonstop, huh?"

"Yup."

"Well," I said, feeling the mood begin to soar, "good thing we're standing in this spot, then."

"Huh?"

I motioned above us, wearing a cheeky grin. Everything about this trip felt like it'd happened how it should, and us landing directly underneath a mistletoe seemed to prove that point. And the way Nick had just opened up to me, bared his soul to me, it pushed me into a whole new territory. I looked into Nick's blue eyes and felt deeply connected to him, like our souls had been tethered together and only now were finding each other, tugging on the invisible and unbreakable rope between us.

And then his lips were on mine, connecting us in an entirely different way.

15 NICHOLAS SILVA

Because *of course* there was a mistletoe directly above us. Because *of course* even the spirit of Christmas was trying to push us together.

I didn't think twice about it. I was done overthinking. I was done dreading every single moment. The outburst and revelation had pushed a thorn right out of my side, one that had been prodding me for far too long. I grabbed Shy, not caring we were in public, and I pulled him in, kissing him with abandon. His warm chest pressed against mine. Heat flooded me. His tongue slipped into my mouth. I grabbed the back of his head, holding him, kissing him.

Claiming him.

I felt so fucking *alive*. That photo Luna had shown me got me pissed, but speaking about my darkest moment with Shy had reminded me what this was all about.

Fuck it all to holiday hell. If someone wanted pictures, they could get it. Videos? Sure, go right ahead. Just make sure you tag me.

Shy fed me a moan, one I swallowed greedily. I wanted more, and judging by the growing length beginning to push against me, I wasn't the only one.

"Let's go to my room," I said against his lips, hand still on the back of his head, my eyes locked with his.

"Let's." He gave me a playful lick before we broke apart, both of us flushed pink with heat. He started to leave the room. I reached for his hand and grabbed it. The both of us froze for a moment, voices starting to drift in our direction from the hall. Instead of letting go, my fingers found better purchase between his. He looked at me, his brows tipped downward. Worry was clear on his face, but I didn't feel it. After talking to Shy, bringing up Hightower, bringing up the hardest fight of my fucking life, it made me realize I would never throw in the towel, and that meant grabbing my man by the hand and walking through the cruise ship together, toward my room where I planned to wreck him until neither of us could see straight.

In the hall were a few other people, all headed to the foam party, none of them paying us any attention as we walked past, hand in hand. I found it a little comical. Sometimes in life, the freshly out-of-the-closet prince of Spain could walk right past you and you'd be none the wiser. As we walked down the hall, we passed the theater, which was currently getting ready to show *The Nutcracker*. People were lined up on the side of the wall, waiting to get in, and we had to walk past all of them, wearing our little swim trunks with our flip-flops flapping, our hands twined together. Here I could feel some eyes land on us. I couldn't tell if the stares were people checking us out or judging us, if anyone knew who I was or didn't.

And yet the bottom line was, I found that I didn't give *any* cruising fucks. I looked to my right, Shiro walking confidently with his chest out and his head up, a cocky little grin on his face. He didn't care either.

The elevator we got into was empty, which was perfect because I couldn't keep my lips off Shy any longer. I kissed him for a moment as the doors shut, barely able to wait until we got to my room. If the wall behind us wasn't pure glass, I would have dropped to my knees and started to blow him.

"Are you ready?" I asked, kissing him again as we rode the elevator up to my floor. "Because I want to worship you until the sun comes up."

"Oh, I'm not planning on sleeping."

I laughed, kissing him again, not caring that the glass elevator didn't hide any of my affection from anyone watching.

"There's a saying in Spain. We call Christmas Eve: *Nochebuena*. And the saying goes: *Esta noche es Nochebuena, y no es noche de dormir.*"

"Okay, I got 'good night,' but that's about it. You speak Spanish so fast!"

"Tonight is the Good Night; it's not a night for sleep."

"Ahh, now I got it." This time Shiro kissed me, leaning up, his smiling lips pressing against mine. "Well, I'm glad we're doing *Nochebuena* right then."

"We're doing it very right," I said, almost purring, feeling myself getting carried away. Thankfully, we weren't in the elevator any longer because I'm sure the glass would have started to steam up any second. The doors opened on my floor. We got out, hands locked together again. My swim trunks were tight against my growing bulge. I shot a glance downward and saw that the head of my cock was clearly outlined against my thigh.

"Someone's excited," Shy said, having followed my gaze. I licked my lips as we stopped in front of my door. I moved his hand so that he cupped my erection.

"Isn't this what you asked for for Christmas? A hung prince from Spain?"

"I thought that was confidential! Fucking Santa, always blabbing shit." Shy shook his head, laughing as he gave me a few gentle strokes. "It's not even Christmas morning, though. Shouldn't I wait to unwrap my gift?"

"We open gifts on *Nochebuena*," I said, kissing him again, making my cock twitch in his grip. "So let's go unwrap yours." Still kissing him, I managed to take out my key card and press it against the lock. The sound of the heavy dead bolt sliding open filled the hall.

Inside my room, I dropped my trunks, revealing nothing underneath except for my already rock-hard cock. Shy didn't waste any time either. He untied his trunks, still a little moist from the foam, and dropped them, also revealing he had gone commando. I grabbed his hips and tugged him in for a kiss, our cocks crossing like two dueling swords, his soft shaft sliding against mine. I thrust, rubbing myself onto him.

"I'm done being scared," I said between breaths. I had to let it be known. Here, when the two of us were naked and connected, I needed Shy to know that I was done. "From this point forward, I'm living my life the way I want to live it." I kissed his smiling lips.

"I'm proud of you, Nick. You deserve to be happy."

"You showed me that, Shy. I hit rock bottom when Luna came to me with that photo. But you pulled me out of it." Another kiss. I felt him throb between us, causing me to do the same. "And you deserve to be happy, too, Shy. You should never have to search for fake friendships or fake relationships ever again." I cupped his head with a gentle hand, pushing a rogue strand of hair from the side of his forehead. "And you certainly don't deserve to find yourself with another potato-chip-addicted bum."

"Who do I deserve to be with, then?" His amber brown eyes pierced through me.

"You deserve to be with a prince."

We collided again, like two comets smashing into one another, creating an explosion big enough to wipe out a planet.

Before the kiss consumed me entirely, I separated from him and turned us around, walking us over to the bedroom. The curtains were all drawn wide open, giving us a stunning view of the moonlit ocean from every room, the balcony wrapping from the living room to the bedroom.

Inside the bedroom, I grabbed Shiro's cock and stroked him a few times, spreading the slick precome up and down his shaft. I loved watched him as his eyes rolled back, the pleasure rocking through him as I thumbed over his wet slit. His knees shook, his lips parted. I fucking loved it.

And I wanted more. Tonight, I wanted it all.

"Bend over." My command cracked like a whip through the room. Shiro didn't take a moment to hesitate. He turned away from me and bent over, placing his hands on the bed, his ass up in the air. His cheeks were spread, exposing him. My arousal rocketed to uncontrollable levels. I reached out and rubbed his cheeks, squeezing them. My cock throbbed in the air, painfully hard, but I ignored my own needs, focusing solely on Shy and his delicious-looking ass.

I gave his left cheek a light slap. "Oooh," he said, moving forward before moving back, giving his ass a wiggle. "Do it again."

Another slap, this one on his right cheek. It wasn't hard and barely left a mark, and Shy seemed to love it. He dropped his head to the bed, arching his back and sticking his ass out even farther. I crouched down, holding both his cheeks. I started to kiss him, nibbling on the sensitive flesh. Shivers rocked through Shy's body—I could feel them as I held on to his thighs.

I wanted to make his entire body quiver, and I had an idea of just how to make that happen.

I spread his cheeks farther apart, his tight hole just begging to be licked. I collected some spit and let it fall down, sliding down his hole, over his balls. I fingered the wet trail, pushing it back up to his hole. Shiro moaned as I thumbed him, feeling the soft ring of muscle clenching.

And then I replaced my thumb with my tongue. Shy jerked forward, gasping in surprise. I grabbed his ass and pulled him back onto my tongue, sliding my tongue up and down his crack.

"Ohhh, Nick! Fuck. Oh, fuck." Shiro had his head down on the mattress, his hands forward and gripping onto the bedsheets. As I ate him out, I reached between his legs, found his stiff cock, and held it tight in my grip.

His entire body spasmed as I prodded him with my tongue. The sensation of holding his hard cock and tonguing his hole almost sent me over the edge, and I hadn't even been paying any attention to myself. I had to pull back because I felt like I was close to coming; it was that intense.

Shiro collapsed onto the bed when I let him go. He started slowly grinding on the mattress, asking for more without saying any words.

I dropped lower in my crouch, letting my knees hit the floor. I lifted him slightly and grabbed his hard dick, and then I brought it between his legs, making sure I didn't hurt him. Judging by the throaty "ohs," I wasn't hurting him in the slightest.

With his dick pulled between his legs, I licked the head, lapping up at the constant flow of precome that leaked out of him. I let his cock go and returned my attention to his hole, licking and lapping, thumbing and prodding.

I couldn't take it anymore. I had to get inside him. I had to fuck him into the goddamn mattress.

But first, I needed something else. Something from Shy.

I stood up, leaving Shy a twitching wet mess on the bed, and walked over to my suitcase. I dug through my underwear and found the bottle and box I was looking for. Shy watched me as I set the lube on the nightstand and tore open a blue condom wrapper with my teeth.

"Mhmm," Shy said as I walked back to the bed. He stuck his ass farther out in the air, and I ached to be buried inside it.

Not yet, though. Instead, I sat down on the bed, Shiro looking at me in surprise.

"I want you to fuck me," I said, pushing the condom in

his direction. His eyes opened wide before he flipped over on the bed, grabbing the condom, a devilish glint in his gaze. "Is that all right? Or are you, you know, strictly a bottom?"

This was all new to me. I wasn't totally sure how it all worked. All I was sure about was that this was the hottest fucking thing to have ever happened to me.

"I'm vers," Shy said as he rolled the condom over his considerable size. "So yes, it's very all right." He laughed as he climbed onto me, kissing me, sucking on my bottom lip, using his teeth to graze the skin. He throbbed against me, and I suddenly realized I asked for that entire size to go inside me.

"You've gotta go slow," I said as Shy trailed his way down my body with his tongue, kissing my pubes, running his tongue around the head of my cock.

"Let's start with these," Shiro said, lifting two fingers in the air. He reached for the lube. I held my cock as I watched him spread the lube around his fingers. He lowered his hands between my legs and slipped the pads of his fingers over my hole.

I twitched backward, surprised at the sensation but immediately wanting more. I closed my eyes as Shiro explored me, rubbing his fingers up and down, getting me nice and slick and ready. It wasn't long before I could feel myself opening up, my muscles relaxing. He told me to take a deep breath, and I did, releasing it the moment his finger slipped inside.

My eyes shot open. "That okay?" he asked, voice gentle.

"Yeah," I said. "Go deeper."

And he did, sending fireworks flying through my vision. I let my head fall back onto the bed as a moan bloomed through my chest, spurred by the sensation of Shy's finger curling inside me, as if coaxing me to come. My cock throbbed in agreement, leaking onto my pubes, my balls tightening against my body.

If Shiro kept going, then a White Christmas was all but guaranteed, and I absolutely didn't want him to stop.

16 SHIRO BROOKS

I was fingering Spanish royalty. Prince Nicholas Silva was asking me to "go deeper" into him, and I was listening, sliding my finger up to the second knuckle, feeling his velvet-soft walls tighten around me. I pushed in, curling my finger, feeling him grip me and pull me in deeper, as if his body cried out for more; the same thing his lips were doing.

"You're so sexy," I said, practically to myself. He ground his ass down on my finger. I pushed another to his hole, and it slipped in with ease. Nick's eyes opened wide. He moved his ass around in a circle, sinking me into him. I gasped, feeling his swollen prostate push against the tips of my fingers. I rubbed.

It looked like Nick had placed his tongue against an electrical socket. He spasmed around my touch, his hands gripping onto the sheets even tighter. I grinned, knowing I had found the spot.

"Holy fuck. *¿Qué hiciste?*" he asked.

"I rubbed your prostate. It's your P-spot. Every guy has it; just not every guy knows how to handle it." I rubbed again, applying more pressure. Nick's eyes rolled. He bit his lips before crying out, his cock throbbing in the air.

In and out, I started to slide, finger fucking him. His cock leaked, making my mouth water. I bent down, still fingering him, holding him with my free hand and aiming his cock up to my lips. I sucked him in.

I slowed down. Judging by how tight Nick's nuts were, he was close to coming, and I didn't want him to blow just yet. So I traced the head of his dick with my tongue, breathing onto it, my fingers working him, stretching him, getting him ready for me.

"Fuck me, Shy." His normally sharp blue eyes seemed glazed over. Lust had taken over. Steam appeared to be rising up from his chest with how fucking hot this was.

I pulled my fingers out, Nick gasping as I did. I pushed him back on the bed, the four solid wood posts rising around either side of us. The bedsheets were silky soft against my knees. I looked to the left, seeing the breathtaking view of the dark ocean, a sickle white moon reflected back on the rippling waters. There was an untouchable serenity to it, somehow making this moment that much more special.

My cock, slick and warm, throbbed in my grip. I lined myself up with Nick, rubbing my head against his hole, his cheeks clenching around me.

"Wait. Here," I said, leaning over and grabbing another

pillow. I lifted Nick and slipped the pillow under him. He watched me with those sultry sea-blue eyes, his lips slightly parted as if stuck in a permanent moan. I broke from his gaze and looked down to admire him. His hard cock pulsed and leaked onto his stomach, covered in a dark shadow of hair.

I pressed myself against his entrance. "Ready?" I asked. The last thing I wanted was to give Nick a terrible first time. I wanted to make sure he was taken care of every step of the way.

"Yes," he said, closing his eyes as I pressed in. His hole opened for me, taking in the head. I could feel him stretch, and the sharp intake of breath made me pause.

"Keep going," he said through gritted teeth.

"Take a breath." I put a hand to his chest. Felt it rise with the breath I had asked for. I pushed in a little farther on the exhale.

"Oh *fuuuuck*, that feels good. Are you in already?"

I looked down, chuckling. "Barely an inch."

"And how much more is there to go?"

"I'd say a good six."

Nick's eyebrows jumped as I went in another inch. "Five now."

"This New Year's countdown sure is very different from the one I'm used to," Nick said, smiling and then gasping as I pushed in deeper. I leaned down, kissing him, chuckling against his lips.

"Wait until the ball drops," I joked, feeling more comfortable than ever before, sharing this moment with Nick.

With his head in my hands and his lips against mine, I fucked him, sinking my complete size into him. He gasped into my mouth. I licked his lips, opening my eyes, his still shut in pure bliss. I leaned back up so that I could hold his legs in the air.

"That all right?" I asked, looking down, his ass clenched around my cock.

"It stings a little," he said. "But keep going. It's getting better."

I listened, pulling back slowly, almost to the tip. And then I rolled forward again, watching myself disappear in Nick, all the way down to my balls. His velvet hot heat wrapped around me. My vision exploded with multicolored stars. I wanted to be crystalized in this very moment for the rest of my life. I would have been more than happy with that happening.

"Shy, *fuck*, you're massive."

"Am I too big?"

"No, I fucking love it." Nick's cock-drunk grin proved he wasn't lying. "Go harder."

I rocked my hips forward, sinking balls-deep. Our grunts and groans turned more and more animalistic as I started to fuck him for real, not holding myself back, letting my body drive. His skin slapped against mine, my balls hitting his ass with every thrust. His head rolled from side to side as I fucked him, his moans rising loud enough to wake up Poseidon himself. It pushed me to fuck him even harder.

"Yes, Nick, *yes*, god your ass feels so fucking good."

He couldn't even get the words out to respond, just gargled something past the grunts he was giving me as I pounded into him, taking his virginity, making his toes curl in the air.

Nick started to shake then. Without any warning, his cock blew, a jet of come shooting out, landing with a splat against the headboard. His hole quivered and pulsed around my cock as I continued to fuck the come out of him, more ropes of his sticky seed shooting out and landing across his chest.

"I'm gonna come, Nick."

"Fuck, do it on me," he said, completely breathless.

I pulled out of him with a pop. I rolled off the condom and aimed myself onto his chest. The sight of him alone, sweaty and covered in come, was enough to make me explode.

I dropped my head back as I came, unloading everything I had on Nick, feeling my muscles start giving out with every shot of come that mixed with Nick's.

By the end of it, Nick looked like I had when I dropped the Frosty cake on top of me. I collapsed onto the bed next to him, my body spent, my cock swollen and limp against my belly, still leaking.

We stayed silent for a few moments, collecting ourselves. It felt like I had transcended, like I had reached some sort of secret level in the Game of Life, one there was no coming back from.

"That was, literally, the best sex of my life," I said, staring up at the white ceiling.

"Really?" Nick asked.

"Yuh."

"Same for me." Nick took a deep breath. "Except, I think I'm starting to cement into one piece."

I looked to my side, laughing as Nick poked at the pool of come on his chest. He lifted his finger and smeared some across my cheek and lips. I gasped in shock before I reached my tongue out and licked some off.

"Let's get showered," Nick said, laughing and kissing me, licking the rest of the come off my face.

"Oh, oh, I'm dripping. I'm dripping." Nick hurried to his balcony door, a hand held underneath him to try and catch any of the drips. I laughed, wondering why he was going to the balcony and not the bathroom. "Come on," he said, as if reading my mind, "this balcony has an outdoor shower."

"Are you... *seriously*? Damn, rich people are spoiled."

I followed him out to the balcony, and sure enough, a small showerhead was installed in the corner of the huge balcony. The balcony's white floors transformed into black-and-white tiles under the shower. A half of a wall covered the side that looked out to the ocean, so you could still shower and admire the view without anyone on shore seeing you below the waist. There was a thin curtain tucked to the side which could be pulled out for further privacy. I didn't care much about it. We were so high up anyway, someone would need binoculars to see what was happening up here.

"This is beautiful," I said, looking out to the sea. Nick started the water and stepped under the stream. I turned to admire an entirely different view.

Nick's body, dripping wet and still flushed from our sex, was an absolute work of art. Good enough to be hung in a museum. The way the balcony light played off the water droplets falling down his muscles mesmerized me. His cock hung heavy and limp. His dark bush, well maintained and tantalizing and soaking wet, crowned him. The shadow of his chest hair was just as drool worthy.

He was making me hard again. I stepped under the shower, the warm water welcome against my skin. The ocean breeze carried the fresh scent of salt and sea, mixing with the vanilla of the soap Nick used to suds up.

We kissed under the water. Nick held me, kissing a smile right onto my face. This felt beyond right. This almost felt destined. Like our meeting and the circumstances leading up to it were predetermined. It was the only way to explain how head over heels I was for this man. How he made my heart race with just a look, and how his body unraveled mine in ways that I didn't even think were possible. Especially not after I had been ready to settle with Mason, thinking that was how good it was ever going to get.

"That was something else." Nick rubbed the suds around his chest. I grabbed the bar of soap and started to wash myself. "I never knew sex could feel so fucking good."

"I'm glad I gave you a good first time."

"Are you kidding? I'm already wanting the second time. And third, and fourth."

I couldn't hold back the smile, or my growing erection.

"Look, I'm still shaking from it," Nick said. He lifted his leg, a small tremble appearing in his thigh. "See? You broke me."

"Sorry, I'll make up for it," I said, turning around with a smile, rubbing my ass up on him. He wrapped his arms around me and rested his head on my shoulder. I rested mine on his. We looked out to the silent ocean as water streamed down on us, and in that peaceful and bliss-filled moment, I knew with a strong certainty that our fates were twined together like a tangle of Christmas lights pulled straight out of storage.

And you know *damn well* those lights are always tangled to infinity and beyond.

I woke up to the smell of coffee in the room, carried on a gentle breeze drifting in through the open balcony door. I stretched under the sheets, feeling the delicious pull of muscles along my thighs, up to my butt. I was naked, having slept like that after Shiro and I drifted off at around four in the morning. We were going to wait for the sunrise, but neither of us could make it. And with the way we had spent last night, I didn't really blame us.

Shiro walked over from the kitchenette, two steaming white mugs of coffee in his hand. He was naked, too, his dick swinging back and forth.

"Morning," I said, trying not to get hypnotized by him.

"Merry Christmas." He flashed me the cheeriest of grins as he got in bed. I perked up.

"Merry Christmas," I said, kissing him and thanking

him for the coffee. It swirled with a dash of sweet cream, exactly how I liked it.

Shy lay on top of the sheets, his head resting on the soft gray leather of the headboard. He crossed his feet at the ankles and looked out at the sea. We had left the dock and were on the way to St. Maarten Island, where we'd spend the next two days. I was excited to explore the island with Shy. Hell, I was just excited to spend an afternoon on the beach with him, excited to do absolutely anything with him. And I was glad that I could spend Christmas with him, too. Being here, on this ship floating across the ocean, it felt more like home than the palace ever did.

"You're special, banana boy."

"And you're annoying, Prince Nick." He angled his face toward me. The morning sunlight seemed to glimmer on his skin as if he'd been sprinkled with gold dust.

"And I'm also officially a hungry bottom after last night," I teased, pushing in for a kiss. Shy smiled, his lips tasting as sweet as the coffee he was drinking. "Seriously, though. You are special, Shy."

"I think you're special, too. You've made this Christmas one I'm never going to forget. Even if I tragically hit my head and suffer a trauma that wipes out all my memory. I'm positive, I'll never forget this Christmas."

I laughed into his neck. "With your track record of falling over, I think I'm going to have to buy you a helmet. Especially if you're going to be jumping on walls the way you do."

"I fell over once. Okay, twice. But that's it."

"There was that one other time..." I trailed off at Shy's

pointed look. "All right, well, just be careful. I don't want my boyfriend forgetting about me."

He looked to me, his lips slanting into a smirk. "Are we talking real boyfriend, here? Or fake?"

"What do you want?"

"As real as it comes."

"Exactly what I want," I said, kissing him over the rising steam of our coffees. "And exactly what I feel, too. For once in my life, I can say I actually feel happy. That probably sounds insane coming out of my mouth. But it's true. I really do feel actual happiness for once."

"It doesn't sound insane at all." Shiro sipped his coffee. "I completely get it. Just because the world sees all the flashy things that come with being a prince, they don't see anything that goes on inside. You were fighting off a storm. No amount of expensive cars or lavish vacations was going to make you feel good, not until you came out."

"Which... I guess I still have to do." I took a deep breath. "I think I'm going to tell my parents today. I don't want them finding out through a photo. I want to tell them myself, and I don't think this can wait for me to get back."

"I think you're right. They should hear it from you. Don't let some dumb ass paparazzo take away your power or your story."

"How should I do it?"

"Just be truthful, say what's in your heart. I know that sounds kinda dumb and fluffy, but it's true. In those situations, you just have to spill your guts. Say it and get it all out there, because once it is, then your job is done." Shy put a hand on my leg. "You've got this. I know you do."

His confidence was nice, seeing as how mine felt

lacking in that moment. I swallowed my nerves, chasing it with a gulp of the coffee.

We talked for a while longer, the conversation drifting to more benign topics. We landed on discussing our star signs again, except this time our conversation felt very different to the one we had in the bookshop.

"Ok, so *now* I'm really going to google if Pisces and Virgos are compatible, and not in the friend way. Not that I really believe in all that but you know, for research," Shy said, laughing as he typed it in.

"And?" I asked, fully invested in the outcome.

"It says... excellent match. Looks like Pisces and Virgos share an emotional connection that others only dream to have. Sourced by... AstrologyAndU.com, spelled with the letter *u*."

"You're a typical Pisces," I said, tsking.

"Oh please, you didn't even know Pisces were the fish."

I shut him up with a cheeky kiss. The kiss grew, as they typically did between us, and we were soon rolling around on the bed, stroking and licking and playing with each other, until Shy's phone started to buzz against the nightstand.

Ace was calling him to come down and hang out with the group. Shy reluctantly pulled off me and said he needed to go down before they thought he'd been abducted or thrown off the side of the ship. I laughed, giving his ass a slap as he got dressed. I told him I would meet them later.

"Are you going to call them now?" he asked as I was saying bye to him at the door.

"I am," I answered, my mouth going as dry as cotton.

"All right, remember, just say what's on your heart.

They're your parents first and foremost—they'll understand where their own son is coming from."

"I hope so."

"I know so." His positivity was welcome, especially when I felt like I was heading toward a massive iceberg. We kissed goodbye and he left, leaving the room in silence.

If I waited any longer, I knew I'd just keep putting it off. I grabbed a shirt and tugged it on. I walked out to the balcony, my pulse pounding. I knew that this was it—this was the moment. I couldn't wait any longer, especially not with that photo still floating around. It could hit at any moment, and there would be no denying it further. I had to come out to my parents.

The FaceTime call had trouble connecting, but once my mom's face popped up on the screen, it was clear and smooth. Rays of sunlight made her silky black hair shine, like some kind of filter had been applied to the video.

"¡Hola, mi hijo! ¡Feliz navidades!"

"Hey, *mamá*. Merry Christmas. Is Dad around?"

"Your father? He is, he is." She walked over to where my father sat at on the ancient couch we had inside the solarium. He sat up and made room for my mom, both their faces filling the screen now. "Everything okay?" my mom asked. Creases appeared around her eyes, revealing the worry she would otherwise have been successful concealing.

"Yes, everything's fine."

"Oh, look who else is here!"

I winced. This was the last thing I needed. Was my mom about to push me onto some other rich girl she found wandering through the rose garden? I couldn't come out if there was an audience. I wanted to talk to my mom and dad alone. Suddenly, the nerves that had nested in my chest prior to the call took full flight, flapping around and rattling my ribs like the bars of a cage. I could feel beads of sweat start rolling down my side, and I usually never sweat.

Before I could freak out any further, my mom flipped the camera and showed who had trotted into the room, a big grin on his golden face, tail wagging like a fan behind him.

"Eli! Hey there, boy."

Maybe he heard my voice or maybe he just got a burst of energy, but something caused him to run forward, straight for the couch where my parents sat. He jumped up, licking my mom's face as the camera flipped back to them.

"So what did you have to talk to us about?" my dad asked. I could tell he sensed something was up. He was good at reading people. I couldn't get anything past him as a kid, and I wouldn't even try to as an adult.

"I don't even know how to start this..."

Fuck. Should I have prepared something? Rehearsed a speech in the bathroom mirror? How did people come out? Why weren't there kids' books explaining this kind of shit? Or at the very least, a "coming out for dummies" book. Anything, so long as it provided even a scrap of guidance.

"You know I love you both, and we've had some rough spots growing up, I know I haven't been the easiest to deal with, but I think there's been a reason for all of that. I've never felt like myself, like I was giving it my all. I always felt like I was playing this... this part. Wearing a mask. It made me sad. Really, *really* sad. That made me angry, and then that made things difficult. But not anymore. I can't live like that anymore. So, that's why, I'm telling you both: I'm gay."

There. The words were out. No taking it back, no reversing things, no changing my mind. I had spoken my truth, and I could do nothing more than stand behind it.

My mom blinked a few times. My dad's face looked set in stone, barely a twitch.

My hand was shaking. I leaned on the balcony, steadying my arm and stopping the shake.

"Gay?" my mom repeated, as if she hadn't heard the first time.

"Sí."

With that, my father snapped out of his stupefaction. He said something I couldn't quite make out, with a tone I'd never heard from him. Something like pure venom. He stood up and left the frame, his heavy footsteps growing farther away. My mom called after him. She stood up, dropping the phone on the couch. Eli, bless him and his golden heart, looked down at the phone, his innocent grin making me feel a little better even though all I really wanted to do was vomit over the balcony.

Less than a minute later, the camera started to move around, my mom's face coming back on the screen. She looked paler than before, and there were strands of hair that hung loose and wild down her forehead. She tucked them behind her ear, swallowed, and said in a shaky voice, "Nicholas. I love you. You're my son, first and foremost, and you always will be."

I let go of a breath I hadn't realized was stuck in my lungs.

"It's just... you're sure? That you're gay?"

"Yes. Very."

"And you don't think you're just—"

"It's real, *mamá*. And it isn't a phase or anything like that. I've been dealing with this since I could remember. And it's hard to say it out loud, and when Dad... It's difficult. So thank you for coming back."

"Of course, *hijo*. I would never abandon you. And your father will come around. I'll talk to him. I don't know what I'll say exactly, but I'll figure that out later."

"Thank you, *mamá*. I'm sorry for having to say this all over FaceTime. I just couldn't hold it in any longer."

She looked down and appeared to be petting Eli. The sun, which had been shining through her hair, caught the glint of a tear slipping from the corner of her eye. "You don't need to apologize. I'm the one who's sorry. I should have known, picked up on something. My motherly instincts never kicked in. Instead, I was pushing girls on you. Without ever thinking twice about what you really wanted."

The emotion in her voice tightened my chest. I could tell she felt apologetic, and I had a feeling that if she could, she would turn back time just to take it all back.

"It's okay," I said, holding back tears. "It's okay now."

"Good," my mom said, stiffening her upper lip. "I just want you to be happy, Nicholas... and now... now things will be so difficult. People are cruel, and the media has already been taking swipes at our family since the start." Her lip quaked before it stiffened again.

"I can handle it. Whatever happens in the tabloids, whatever happens online, none of it matters. All I care about is you and dad. And, at the end of the day, if I could use my story to help out at least one closeted kid out there, then all the pain and shit-talking would be worth it."

"Spain is still such a religious country."

"Then they'll need to actually practice what they preach and love their neighbor as they'd love themselves. Leave the judgment for judgment day."

My mom chuckled, but the worry lines didn't disappear from her face. If anything they had multiplied.

"We'll be okay. I'll be okay," I reiterated, with a little more force this time.

"I know, Nicholas. I have no doubt about that." She choked back a cry. "When did you know?"

"Since the day I got butterflies meeting the president's son."

"You were... that was when you were barely ten."

"I probably even knew before then. I've fought it—trust me, I've fought it. But it was useless. I was only beating up on myself at the end of the day."

My mom's smile grew. "No more of that."

"No more."

She stood up from the couch. I could hear Eli jump off to follow her. "I'll go talk to your father. He just needs some time to process it. Call me if anything, okay? *Te amo*, Nick."

"I love you, *mamá*."

And just like that, it was done. A flip had been switched. Everything was real, and there was no turning back now, no more running and no more hiding.

I was free.

18 SHIRO BROOKS

We all raised our glasses, the sound of our cheers lifting up to the cloudy night sky.

"To friendship!" we sang out, clinking the glasses. My toes sunk into the sand underneath me as I drank my beer, my heart feeling full as I looked around the table of friends, reunited after all those years. We sat out on the beach of St. Maarten, celebrating Christmas with a large dinner and endless drinks. There were dozens and dozens of circular tables set around the sand, with music playing and a dance floor beginning to form. The sun was setting, the early rays of its purple and orange light starting to fill the sky.

The only thing this scene missed was Nick, who had said he wasn't feeling too great and had to skip out on dinner. He said he would join for drinks, but there was still no sign of him, and I started to get worried. I knew he wanted to speak to his parents when I had left his room... Had something happened? What if he called it quits on us and I didn't even know. I was just sitting here, toes in the sand, drink in my hand, none the wiser that another breakup was headed my way.

"Where's your new boyfriend?" Jada asked, probably reading the worry that I felt flash across my face. "Everything all right with him?"

"Yeah, I think so." It felt weird referring to Nick as my "boyfriend." The title was as new as our relationship.

"Don't they make such a cute couple," Ace chimed in.

Lou sat up in his seat. His cell phone–addicted girlfriend sat next to him, munching on some bread and scrolling through her phone. "I don't think I remember ever seeing you smile that big," he said, pointing at the grin that manifested itself every time Nick's name was brought up.

Jada nodded and played with the hem of the white tablecloth covering the table. "Yeah, I loved you and Mace, but I could tell things weren't exactly perfect. I just didn't really see the spark. But with Nick, I saw the spark even before you told us anything. From day one, I had some suspicions. Right, Ken?"

"Yup. The second we got into our room, she said that you two were looking at each other funny."

"And the energy coming off the two of you. I just knew." Jada let go of the tablecloth and sat back in her chair. "And I was right."

"He seems like a really good guy, too," Rex offered, speaking in his low baritone. "I spent some time with him by the pool. He left a great impression on me."

"Speaking of the sexy devil," Ace said, pointing with his chin toward the entrance to the beach.

Nick walked toward us. He wore white pants and a navy blue button-down, his sandals dangling in his hand as he kicked up sand behind him. He smiled at the table and gave everyone a wave, but I stood up and went over to him. The second we kissed, the table behind us erupted in cheers.

I rolled my eyes. "Everything okay?" I asked, smiling, happy that Nick hadn't secretly packed up and escaped on another boat.

"Not exactly."

My heart dropped. "Come on, let's talk over by the water."

Hands entwined, we walked over to the edge of the water, where the ocean lapped up onto the sand in foamy turns. The waves were almost nonexistent. We sat down on the dry sand, putting our feet onto the wet side, letting the warm waters rise up to meet us.

"I spoke to my parents," Nick said, his gaze turned out to the fire-orange horizon.

"And? How did it go?" I didn't want my nerves to show, so I sat on my hands in case I started to chew on my fingernails.

"My mom took it well. She just thinks the world will be a thousand times harder now. She doesn't realize how difficult it was for me before, and how easy it all seems now. But she will, though. That'll come with time. I'm just glad she's started that process of accepting already."

"Good, yeah. My mom was the same way when I came out. She cried not because I was gay, but she said it was because she pictured me getting hurt. Beaten up *for* being gay. I told her that she doesn't have to worry. I've got a good head on my shoulders and can run like a gay bat out of glittering hell if it ever came down to it."

Nick laughed at that. I stopped sitting on my hand and instead reached for his.

"And your dad?"

"That didn't go as well..." Nick shook his head, still looking out at the sea. "It didn't really go at all. I spilled my guts out and told them how I felt, and he, well, just walked off. He got up and left. I didn't think he'd do that. I thought he'd at least say something so that I could talk him down. But he didn't even give me that chance. He just... left."

I squeezed Nick's hand. "Fuck... Nick. He just needs time. He'll come around."

"That's what my mom said, but I don't know. His expression... I don't think I've ever seen him like that. I know what he's thinking, too: How will I inherit the crown? Does the bloodline end with me? I'm sure that's what he's focused on."

"Maybe a hundred years ago it would have ended with you, but science can do all kinds of things these days. Not only can kids make glow-in-the-dark slime now, but gay guys can have kids, too. And it's not like you don't have money for surrogacy." I nudged into Nick's shoulder.

"Do the kids come glow-in-the-dark, too?"

"I think you have to pay extra for that feature."

Nick chuckled. I could tell he felt better having said his truth, but the worry about his dad wasn't going anywhere.

"It'll be hard," he said. "Spaniards love tradition, and this throws tradition out the window."

"Well, things change. People will come around. Maybe you can start an entirely new tradition. One of, I don't know, acceptance? That'd be nice."

"That would be nice, wouldn't it?"

"Yup."

Nick leaned in and kissed my cheek. It caught me by surprise. I looked his way, the both of us smiling. He leaned in and kissed me again, this time on the lips. When we parted, his blue eyes seemed to have a sudden storm in them.

"What will happen to us?" he asked, biting on his lower lip. "After this cruise."

It was a question that had kept me up for the past few nights. I hadn't really thought much of it when Nick and I were rolling around naked and having the time of our lives, but then reality would hit and I'd realize that this trip was quickly coming to an end and we would both be headed in totally different directions.

"I've got a ton of airline miles I've been meaning to use," I said.

"And I have a private jet I can take whenever I want to."

"Because of course you do," I smirked, narrowing my eyes, "Prince Nick."

"Did you expect anything less, banana boy?" He kissed me again. It sent little shocks coursing through my body. We were out in public, and Nick was kissing me, in front of plenty of eyes that could be looking our way.

"We're going to make it work," said Nick, conviction in his tone. "I really feel connected to you, Shy, in a way I've never felt before. And it's not just because our relationship is shiny and new. I see way past that. I see how well we click, how everything just flows when you're next to me. It doesn't feel like I'm swimming upstream anymore, fighting the current. And, honestly, I thought that I'd want to go down the 'app' route and hook up with random guys, but I really don't want any of that." His foot playfully bumped mine. "All I want is you."

"For Christmas?"

"And Easter, and Thanksgiving, and fucking Flag Day."

"What'd you just call me?"

Nick and I both cracked up, the warmth of the moment flowing over me, cementing the feelings I had for this spectacular man at my side.

"I feel the same exact way," I said, my heart unlocking and its contents spilling out. "I really did think I was set for a mediocre life. I thought I would be with Mason forever, living in our cramped one-bedroom apartment, him never cleaning or cooking or helping in any kind of way. I was totally okay with settling for a jobless hamster, basically. And not even a cute hamster. He's one of those hamsters with the draggy butts. And I was ready to call it a day and spend the rest of my life with him. Then he broke things off, and I really thought I was meant for nothing or nobody special. I dreaded this cruise, even though it meant reuniting with all my friends. I wasn't even excited for Christmas, and I freaking loved Christmas." Something in the distance jumped out of the water, too quick to discern what it was. A small splash immediately followed. "You know, I had even thought of canceling? I was literally *seconds* from texting the group and saying that I had gotten in a bad car wreck and couldn't make it. On the way there, I was about to do it. Instead, I sucked it up and showed up. And then I met you." My grin was so wide it hurt my cheeks. "My real-life Prince Charming... and then I asked you to be my fake boyfriend, and you said no."

"Sorry about that," Nick said, kissing me with a grin on his face, too. "But isn't real boyfriends so much better?"

"It is, it is. I wouldn't change how things went down, not one part of it."

"Good. Neither would I."

I leaned and rested my head on Nick's shoulder. The sun was halfway gone now, throwing its rays of last light across the serene waters. The sounds of the party behind us seemed to dim, taken over by the music of our beating hearts, synced together in spectacular fashion.

We stayed like that, watching as the sun disappeared, connected to each other in a way that felt unbreakable.

"We should get back to the table," I said, straightening up, stretching my neck, cracking my knuckles. I wiggled my toes as another wave gently crawled up the beach, foaming around the heel of my foot.

"*Vamos*," Nick said. I had to get him to speak Spanish more often around me, because even just one word flooded my basement.

We stood up, both of us stretching and wiping the sand off our butts. Tiki torches had been turned on, their tall flames illuminating the party. My friends still sat at the same table, an assortment of empty glasses sitting next to their refilled glasses, Ace waving me over as he spotted us walking back.

I looked past the table, seeing Luna standing by one of the tiki torches, wearing her usual black slacks and billowy shirt. I didn't think much of it until I took a closer look at the two people she was talking to.

A woman, who had the same straight, jet-black hair as Luna, and a man, whose bald head caught the flickering light of the torch, his face fully visible and not covered by any shadows. He had a round face with a birthmark across his hand, a birthmark that had been missing from the man I talked to at the market.

"Hey, Nick, who's Luna talking to right now? Over by that tiki torch."

Nick looked, answering instantly. "Those are her parents. Her mom and stepdad."

"Holy fuck," I said, and walked right past my table of friends. Nick followed right on my heels.

"What? What happened?"

"Her stepdad. That's the man I saw during the ugly sweater party, the one I chased after. Luna's stepdad was the one who took our photos. And that's why she got that accidental text. He must have been talking to her right before he tried to sell our photos and sent them to her instead of his magazine connection."

"*Hijo de puta.*"

I nodded, feeling my adrenaline rush as we got closer. "Yeah, exactly."

Luna looked our way, her head cocked to the side and her eyebrows meeting at the center of her forehead. She looked to me, then to Shy, then to her parents.

"Hi, Luna," Shy said, waving before turning to her stepfather. He was a tall man with a permanent scowl on his face. He had married Luna's mother about five years ago. I remember meeting him one time at the palace and never feeling very good vibes from him, but it certainly wasn't my place to comment on Luna's family matters.

"Nick, what's going on?" Luna asked.

"I think we should ask your stepdad that question." Shy crossed his arms. His muscles pushed against the dark red polo he wore. "We've been having some issues with photos being sold to the tabloids, and I've been trying to figure out who's the one involved. I really thought it would be impossible to figure out, but then Luna got that text message."

"Are you accusing me of something?" The stepfather—Henry was his name—took a step forward. I puffed my chest, ready to throw a fist if it came to it. Luna also tensed. I could tell she was getting ready to jump in, but was still listening intently. Her mom stood to the side, confused as all hell.

"Why did you run from me at the sweater party? After I had seen the flash go off on your phone?"

"I didn't run anywhere." Henry spoke with a heavy Spanish accent. "I needed to find the bathroom."

Shiro tilted his head back. He didn't believe him, and neither did I. "You bolted, and you went away from the bathrooms. You were clearly trying to lose me in the crowds."

"So what? If I want a picture of the party, I can get one."

"Show me your phone." Shiro held his hand out.

"No." He put his hands in the pocket of his cargo shorts, as if blocking us from reaching in.

"Show us your phone and it'll solve everything."

Luna shook her head. "This is a little crazy. I don't think—"

"Show them the phone, Henry." It was Luna's mom, Theresa. Her lips were held in a tight line, almost as narrow as the eyebrows she'd drawn on. "I've been seeing strange numbers on his phone." She was speaking to us, Henry looking at her with a dumbfounded expression. "I've noticed him taking a lot of photos. More than usual. I didn't think he was selling them, but... Show us the phone, Henry."

"*¿En serio?*" he asked her.

"Very serious."

For a hair of a second, I thought he was going to run again. I half expected him to bolt, making Shiro and I run after him. He must have been hit with common sense at the last minute since he stayed put and pulled out his phone. With the way he was resisting, I knew we were about to find something. If it wasn't a stash of photos he had taken of me, then it would probably be a stash of nudes he'd been collecting from a mistress. One or the other, Henry acted guilty before he even unlocked his phone for us.

Luna grabbed it first and went straight for the text messages. "There's nothing here. He didn't send that picture to me."

"Maybe he deleted the text," I suggested.

"Or," Shy said, taking his turn with the phone, "he's got it hidden somewhere..." He poked at the screen, thumbing through the pages of unorganized apps filling up the phone. It didn't take him much longer to go, "Aha." I watched all the color from Henry's face drain. He was caught, and he knew it.

"Look at this."

Shiro handed me the phone. It was an app that generated new numbers for anyone using it. In it was a text message sent to a contact, and that message contained a photo of Shy and me. It was the same message Luna had received.

"Fucking bastard." I showed the phone to Luna and Theresa, both of them looking at Henry with intense disappointment in their eyes.

"Why, Henry?" It was Theresa. "You know the kind of

hell Nicholas goes through. Why would you be one of the leeches who puts him through it? And on a vacation that Luna tells us is supposed to be private?"

"It was good money." Henry let his shoulders slump. He had nowhere to run now, and he had no more photos to sell. I'd make sure of that.

"Well," I said, turning to face the ocean, "use that money to buy you a new phone." I let the phone fly, throwing it as hard as I could. I watched it splash into the ocean, the tide tugging it deeper into the darkness. Henry shouted a curse but didn't run after it. He just put both hands on his face while Theresa gave him a slap over the head.

"And that's too bad. You probably would have wanted to capture this up close." I turned back to Shy and grabbed his head in my hands. I gave him the sloppiest kiss I could have, making sure it was clear that tongue and spit was involved. It may have been a little over-the-top, but fuck it, I felt like this was the perfect way to end this messy paparazzo saga.

Besides, there was nothing else I could do. Maybe legal action, except the damage was already done, and I also didn't want to negatively affect Luna or her mom either. Let Henry learn from his lesson and be banned from the palace for the rest of his life.

Done and done.

"All right. I'm going to go enjoy the rest of my Christmas." I wiped the shine off my lips. Shy looked a little shocked, but the smile playing on his face told me he quite enjoyed closing this case.

As we started to leave, Henry and Theresa went off in

the direction of the ship, the two of them loudly arguing. Luna walked with us back to the table where Shy's friends were sitting.

"Nicholas, I'm so sorry. I never would have even imagined... I shouldn't have let that slide."

"It's all right, Luna. Shit happens. I'm just glad we've plugged up this leak. I can enjoy the rest of the cruise now."

"Okay, good... And Shiro, when you interviewed me, I didn't even bring them up because, well, I really wouldn't expect one of them being involved."

Shy waved a hand in the air. "I should have dug a little deeper. We both dropped the Christmas ornament on this one."

Luna pursed her lips. As we reached the table, I could tell she was about to keep walking, most likely to stand a few feet away so she could keep watch over me discreetly. Shiro stopped her before she could go.

"Hey, guys."

The table quieted down and looked to Shiro, who had Luna's hand in his. "This is Luna. She's a friend of mine and just so happens to be Nick's undercover guard. He needs it, considering he's the prince of Spain and all. So, yeah, everyone, meet Luna!"

His friends all stared for a moment before the table broke out into laughter. Shy laughed, too, finally saying, "No, guys, I'm being totally serious right now."

Ace was the first to break out of the stunned spell. "I fucking knew it!" He clapped his hands and stood up, pointing at Rex. "This one here said that maybe you were someone from an oil family, but nope, I called royalty!" He flipped his hand and opened his palm. Rex, with a defeated grin, pulled out his wallet and slapped it on Ace's palm. Ace opened the cracked brown leather wallet and pulled out a fifty.

"Thanks, babes." He kissed Rex before sitting down, pocketing his win. The rest of the gang still appeared stunned. Lou blinked a few times, his girlfriend typing away furiously on her phone before lifting up and saying, "He isn't lying," with a picture of me and my family on her screen, the palace rising behind us.

A deluge of questions fell on me then. All at once. I tried answering them, but it was futile. The dam had broken. We spent a good twenty minutes covering the bare basics of life as a prince, but the questions were just not stopping.

Shy was able to press pause. "Okay, all right, guys. We'll continue this Prince Silva meet and greet in fifteen minutes. Let us go get drinks first. We've gotta fuel up," he said, interrupting as Jada started to ask me how the crown was cleaned. Luna took over the questions as we excused ourselves.

We walked through the sand, over to the bar that sat tucked inside of a straw hut.

"That was kind of you," I said, leaning against the polished wood as the bartender worked on making someone else's drink. "To introduce Luna to the group."

"I figured her Christmas was turning out pretty shitty, I didn't want her standing off to the side all by herself. And I also figured it would be a great way to just drop the news on them about you being a prince. They were going to find out eventually."

I leaned in for a kiss. "It worked out perfectly." I

looked back at the table. Luna was laughing and chatting with Jada and Nick. Lou danced with his girlfriend next to the tiki torch, twirling her around as the music picked up. Ace and Rex were being very touchy-feely with a handsome olive-skinned bartender they seemed to have lured out from behind the bar and who was now sitting on Rex's lap as Ace appeared to be giving him a hand massage.

"Who would have thought this would be how our Christmas played out," Shy said, bumping into my side.

"Certainly not me. I had no idea what to expect when I boarded the ship."

Before I could order our drinks, my phone started to buzz. I thought maybe it was some family member or friend back at home calling to wish me a merry Christmas.

The name on my screen made me freeze. Shy looked at the phone, his eyes opening wide.

Above the picture of the smiling man who looked a lot like me was written the word "Papa."

"I've got to answer this," I said, feeling the nerves rocket up inside me all over again. Shiro nodded and said of course as I stepped to the side, the wind picking up just then and rustling the leaves of a palm tree just behind me.

"*Hola, Papa,*" I said as the call connected. My heart beat terribly hard. Shy wasn't that far from me. I looked to him in an attempt to calm myself down.

"*Hola, hijo.*" It didn't work. My heart beat even harder if that were possible. His expression was hard to read and slightly pixelated. I could see a seriousness in his blue-gray eyes and the barest ghost of a smile on his lips.

He still called me son.

"Listen, about earlier," I started, wanting to end this tension once and for all.

"No. Let me speak."

Oh shit. Okay.

I quieted down, like I was a seven-year-old boy again being scolded by his father for shouting at the fancy fundraising dinner.

"Nicholas, your news shocked me. It came from nowhere and took me by complete surprise. I'm not used to that. I know about everything that goes on around me, at all times. I have eyes and ears behind every door. And yet, somehow, I missed this. I missed the fact that my son was hurting."

Behind my father, I could see the painting of Sierra Blanca he had hanging in his office. It was a painting I had commissioned for him as a fiftieth birthday gift by his favorite artist of the stunning mountain range, its limestone facade depicted in beautiful bold strokes of paint.

"I should have known," he continued. "Should have sensed something was going on with you."

"You couldn't have known. I worked hard to keep it a secret."

"Which makes me even sadder for you, son. And the way I reacted. It came from my own fears and prejudices, not from your news itself. I'm sorry for that, Nicholas."

"It's okay," I said, swallowing a sudden lump in my throat. This was the first time I'd ever heard my dad apologize about anything. He never said sorry, not to anyone. Even when he sorely needed to, he had never said it.

He cleared his throat. "I still have a lot to digest. It will be a process for me, I can't say it will be the easiest thing in the world. But, what I can say, Nick, is that I love you unconditionally. Nothing will change that."

That was it. What I'd been needing to hear from my father. The words that soothed my soul like an aloe vera balm applied to a fresh burn.

"Thank you, Dad. I know it's a lot to take in, but—" I couldn't keep speaking. My voice cracked and emotion welled up, threatening to take complete control.

"But I'll manage," he said, picking up where I left off. "So long as my family is still whole, that's all that matters. I spoke to your mother, and we've already come up with a plan on how to handle the press. The church will be a different matter entirely, but we'll tackle that, too. I won't disappoint you, son."

That struck deep. I nodded, knowing I couldn't get any words out without turning into a sobbing mess.

"The blood that flows through you hasn't changed, Nicholas. Nothing about you has changed. Except for your glow. That smile. I haven't seen you smile like that in what feels like years. How can I ever do anything to compromise that kind of happiness for my own son? I would be a heartless coward, not a worthy king. I won't abandon you, Nicholas. *Te amo, mi niño.* And I will always love you. Gay, straight, bi, or whatever color of the rainbow you fall on."

That was it—all I needed for the tears to spill over like a flooded riverbank. I nodded and wiped at the flow but couldn't stop it. It was so intense, I had to wave Shy over and hand him the phone for a moment while I collected myself.

This went beyond everything I thought I needed. It went back to being a child and just wanting my dad's approval, knowing deep down that there would always be something stopping him from giving it to me in its entirety. And yet, that assumption had been proven wrong. So, so fucking wrong. My dad was giving me his approval, the real me. He knew the real me, and he accepted me. Loved me.

I pulled it together and grabbed the phone back, thanking Shy, who gave me a reassuring back rub before stepping to the side.

"Dad, there's someone I want you to meet."

Shy's eyes opened wide, a small shake in his head telling me "no, no, that's okay," but I grabbed him anyway and pulled him into the shot. He smiled at the camera and gave a friendly wave.

"Hi there."

"And this is?"

"This is Shy—he's my boyfriend."

My father's ghost of a smile solidified, his face transforming completely when he wore a smile. He had one of the kindest faces ever, so long as his eyes crinkled and his dimples appeared.

"Please to meet you, Shy. I'm Ricardo."

"Nice to meet you, Ricardo. Eh, King Ricardo. King Silva. Mr. Silva. Mr. King Si—"

"Ricky is fine," my dad said, laughing as Shy's cheeks turned as red as rosebuds.

"All right, Dad, I'll let you go. Thank you for calling me. It really means a lot. Coming out is the scariest thing I've ever done, and now I can see that it's also the most worthwhile thing, too."

"Of course, Nick. You deserve happiness, and you already seemed to have found it." And through the pixels, I realized then that my father had shed tears of his own, a rogue glint of wetness shining at the corner of his face before he brushed it away.

"Goodbye, *hijo*, and *Feliz Navidades*."

"*Feliz Navidades*, Dad."

Shiro shouted a merry Christmas from off-screen. My dad gave a friendly wave before another tear slid down his cheek. The call ended, his image freezing on his big grin before cutting to black again.

I looked to Shiro, feeling both exhausted and relieved and ecstatic, all in one nerve-racked package. I pulled him in for a kiss and held him against me.

"I can feel your heart beating through your shirt," Shy said, putting his hand against my chest and looking up at me.

"I've never been more scared."

"I'm so glad he came around to the rainbow side. I told you he would just need time. Thankfully it wasn't too much time."

I kissed the top of his head. The deliciously fruity scent of his shampoo filled my nose. "My mom has a way with words. I'm sure she worked her magic."

"Yeah, but I think your dad would have come around regardless. His love for you is obvious. He wouldn't have been upset for long."

"Thank you for being there for me, too."

Shiro looked up at me, the light of the torch dancing in the pools of his golden brown eyes. "Of course, Nick. I've got your back. Always."

"Always?"

"Always."

I couldn't keep my lips off him. I kissed him again before saying, "And I've got yours."

"Oh get a room, you two!" shouted a voice from off to the side. We both looked, seeing Ace and Rex walking away, the cutie bartender walking in between them, all three of them with their arms looped behind the other. "And when you do, give us that room number! We'll be over with our party of three," Ace said over his shoulder with a wink, sticking his tongue out.

They left toward the ship, leaving me and Shy laughing, Shy's cheeks blushing again.

"Looks like they're gonna have a good night," Shy said.

"And I plan on having an even better one." I grabbed him and dipped him, kissing him, claiming him right there on the beach. In that moment, I had zero doubt about one thing:

This Christmas truly turned out to be one for the books.

EPILOGUE

ONE YEAR LATER

Shiro Brooks

I kissed Nick softly, on the cheek first before pecking my way to his lips. He gave a tired little groan and stretched under the covers before flipping over, his naked body pressing against mine as he threw an arm over me and pulled me into him, stopping the kisses. I slipped into little-spoon mode and curled my body into his, crossing my ankles with him. His erection throbbed against my ass, making my own morning wood twitch in response. I looked out the open window of his bedroom, the morning sunlight filling the space, causing tiny dust motes to pop like sparkles in the air. Outside, the winter sky was cloudless, an expanse of azure stretching out for what seemed like infinity from my vantage point on the bed.

"Good morning," Nick said sleepily into the back of my head.

"Merry Christmas, babe."

"*Feliz Navidades*," Nick replied, sounding slightly more awake.

His hand traveled the length of my side, stopping on my hip, his fingers just inches away from my cock.

I flipped back over, facing him, our dicks rubbing together. I pushed my thigh between his, feeling his balls press against my skin. I smiled and kissed him again. I knew I could never get tired of waking up like this. It had been close to a month since Nick and I had slept naked and in the same bed together. Ever since our relationship began, we both worked hard to make sure not a lot of time passed until we saw each other again. Nick would fly me out to Spain or he'd fly to Miami, or we'd end up flying somewhere entirely new together. So long as we were together, then it didn't really matter where we were.

It helped that we didn't care about the paparazzi anymore. I didn't have to worry about sneaky shots, since there were already plenty of photos of us kissing. It meant Luna's dad had to go find a new gig (and a new wife, since Theresa dumped his sketchy ass).

This morning was extra special. Not only was it Christmas and I was waking up in Nick's arms, looking out at the view of a beautiful palace rose garden dusted in pristine white snow, but it was also our one-year anniversary. It was last Christmas that Nick and I became official, marking the beginning of the best year of my life.

I kissed him again, the memory warming my heart. Under the covers, we both were rubbing each other, softly, lazily. I had my hand around Nick, and Nick had his hand around me, his thumb crossing over my slit and sending mini shock waves exploding down my spine.

"Happy one-year anniversary," I said playfully as I leaned up, opening my legs a little wider under the covers as Nick's stroking became more vigorous. He rubbed our two tips together, making my eyes roll and my lips part.

"Happy anniversary, baby." Nick, the mischievous horny prince that he was, went under the covers, disappearing as his kisses started to brush against my skin, trailing downward, over my stomach, down to the base of my hard length. It looked like I had been trying to smuggle the Eiffel Tower under Nick's white bedsheets. There was a small wet spot growing from where I leaked as Nick's tongue massaged my balls.

I threw the bedsheets off me, having to watch as Nick popped one of my balls into his mouth. He smiled at me from between my legs as he sucked, rolling my nut gently between his lips, flicking his tongue across my skin.

I stretched my legs out and curled my toes. Nick's room was on the fourth floor and the bed was pushed away from the window, so even though I could see out, I knew that no one could see in.

"I've missed you," Nick said, his breath tickling my inner thighs. He moved to my other nut, sucking and playing with it.

"I missed you, too, Nick." I dropped my head on the fluffy pillow, already wishing I didn't have to leave. I had flown in three days ago and was only supposed to say for another three, but I was seriously considering extending my trip. Maybe I could stay until next Christmas?

Nick's tongue traced up my shaft, his warm breath sending shivers through me. He popped me into his mouth and looked up at me, wearing a grin as he swallowed my cock, going all the way down to my balls in one go. I moaned, biting on a knuckle before I got too loud. I never knew when someone was walking just outside the door, and with Nick between my legs, I had a tendency of getting loud enough to be heard even through a closed door.

His head bobbed up and down as he worked me. I loved how hungry he looked. How he seemed to love sucking me off as much as I loved it. It drove me absolutely crazy with desire, frying all my circuits with a blazing hot heat.

And then Nick did something else that sent me completely over the edge. He stopped sucking on me and went back to licking, tracing his tongue down my shaft, over my balls. There, he lifted my sac, and his tongue went back to work, making stars shoot across my vision. I writhed on the bed as Nick's tongue flicked over the sensitive bridge of flesh and down toward my pulsing hole. My balls were resting on his face as he flicked his tongue up and down. I returned the knuckle back between my teeth as another loud and uncontrollable moan threatened to escape me

When he came up for breath, I took that moment to truly admire him. His strong shoulders, sinewy with muscles that broadened his shape, twitched as he held himself up, his lips shiny and wet. He was on the bed and kneeling between my legs, so I could see his hard dick swinging between his thighs, his heavy balls looking like they needed to be emptied.

And I knew exactly how I could make them blow.

"Come here," I said, moving down on the bed so that our cocks were pushed back together again and my feet dangled off the edge. I grabbed Nick and kissed him, tasting myself on his tongue. It was an intoxicating mix that only made me more drunk off our love.

"I want to fuck you." The words came out of me in a growl. Before Nick and I got together, I had considered myself a vers, enjoying both giving and receiving. But since Nick, I found that all I really loved to do was top him. The way his body fit around mine made me transcend every single time we made love. I couldn't get enough of his perfect, bubbly ass. Of being inside it. I reached around him and squeezed, emphasizing my words.

Nick didn't waste any more time. He rolled off me and went to the nightstand, the one away from the window. He opened the top drawer and pulled out the small black bottle of lube. I admired him as he pumped some onto his open hand, my gaze drawn down to his hard cock, the sexy tuft of dark hair sitting above his thick base like a crown.

"Finger yourself, Nick."

He licked his lips, smirking as he reached behind himself.

"But turn around. I want to see."

Nick listened to me, turning so that he faced the mirror sitting on the dresser, leaning slightly forward. We made eye contact in the reflection. His eyebrows shot up as he slipped a finger inside himself. He used his other hand to spread his ass, giving me a better view of the way his finger disappeared up to the second knuckle.

"Fuuuuck," I let out on a breath. I moved so that I sat off the edge of the bed, facing Nick. My cock throbbed as Nick's finger went in even deeper, pushing up against his knuckle. Nick let out a small gasp. I could tell he was swirling his finger, massaging his prostate. I started to jerk off, watching Nick push in another finger, this one slipping in just as deep as the first. Nick's hole stretched around him. He groaned, dropping his head as he found his spot, his hand letting go of his cheek and instead holding the dresser in front of him.

He started to go faster. I mimicked his pace. Morning sunlight splashed over his back, highlighting the rippling muscles that danced as he moved. His full balls swung underneath him. I jerked off faster, the sound of his wet and hungry ass sending me to the fucking moon.

"I have to have you." I stood from the bed, unable to hold back anymore. The only thing I wanted in this world was to sink into Nick, that was it.

He pulled his fingers out with a moan. He held his cheeks open for me as I reached around him and grabbed the lube from the dresser. I managed not to drop the slippery bottle as I pumped some onto my hard cock. I set it back down and returned my hand to my shaft, spreading the lube, my knees trembling at the added silkiness.

"Do it, baby. Fuck me." Nick rubbed his ass back, emphasizing his words.

I held the base of my cock and pressed it against his hole. He took in a sharp breath as I pushed in, his body not offering any resistance. His intense heat enveloped me. I sank in farther, overwhelmed with pleasure, relishing every single inch of sensation. Nick had both hands on the dresser. In the mirror, I watched as his face broke with ecstasy, my cock sinking all the way into him.

I rubbed his back, holding his hips. I leaned down and kissed the back of his neck, our bodies turned one.

"God, I fucking love you," I said, kissing him, slowly moving my hips back.

"I love you, too, Shy. So much." Nick looked into the mirror, a wicked grin on his face. "Now fuck me harder."

Nicholas Silva

Having Shy inside me felt like heaven. It had to be what heaven felt like. His cock was the perfect size, thick enough to stretch me and long enough to hit every spot I needed. He knew exactly how to move his hips, too. Rocking into me slowly at first before he picked up the pace, his cock sliding in and out of my needy hole. My fingers turned pale as I grabbed the edges of the ancient dresser, trying hard not to shout out in pure bliss as Shy started to fuck me with abandon.

His balls slapped against me, his cock pummeling me. I wanted to cry out but swallowed it at the last moment, shutting my eyes and biting on my bottom lip instead. My cock bounced with the force of Shy rocking into me.

"Oh fuck, fuck, you're so fucking tight." His words were low and gravelly. I loved when he took control like this. When his fingers dug into the sides of my hips, pushing me down on him. I tightened around him, pulling him in deeper. Shy moaned, loud enough to be heard if someone were to walk by.

At that point, I was so dick drunk, I didn't really care. I continued to squeeze as Shy continued to fuck me, his cock filling me.

The mirror started to wobble. I knew it was time to move to the bed. I put a hand behind me, on his hip, slowing his thrusts. With a moan from the both of us, Shy pulled out of me. I immediately felt empty.

"Sit down," I said, pointing at the bed. Shiro walked over and sat, watching me with his beautiful brown eyes, lit up like a crystal glass of whiskey set on fire. He looked stunning. Literally fucking stunning. His cock was hard and slick, shining in the sunlight, throbbing in his grip. His chest was flushed, muscular and hard, his nipples perked. And those abs of his, *coñoooo*. I could stare at them all day and not get bored.

But it was his cock I focused on. I walked over to him, reaching the bedside, stopping when our toes touched. I smiled down at him and started stroking him, spreading the lube around. Then I climbed onto the bed, squatting onto him, the tip of his cock pushing against my hole as I lowered myself.

Both our mouths drew into the shape of an O. I sat down, taking him in all the way. The pressure of having him inside me was addictive.

Shy fell back onto the bed. I started to ride him, up and down, placing both my hands on his chest. We started to sound like wild animals, our sounds being pushed out with the force of Shy fucking into me. I grabbed my dick, stopping it from bouncing, and started to jerk, feeling myself getting closer and closer to the edge.

Shiro's love-drunk gaze told me he was getting close, too.

"Fuck, baby, keep riding me like that," he said, the pleasure dripping off his tone.

"I'm getting close," I warned, the pressure building inside my balls.

"Do it, Nick. I want you to shoot all over me."

I rode him slow and deep, relishing in every inch of him sinking into me, pushing against my swollen prostate. It was all I needed. My head tilted back, and my orgasm slammed through me. I shot my load, my balls emptying all over Shy, ropes of come shooting across his chest, thick and white, some dripping off his chin. I looked down, my body twitching, and I watched as Shy reached his peak with me. He bucked into me and held himself there as he came, filling me up with his come.

In a heap, I collapsed onto him, not caring that I got sticky and wet with him. We kissed through our smiles, pecks at first, evolving into something more. He was still inside me, his dick growing soft before falling out. I stayed on top of him, looking down into dreamy eyes, a pair of eyes that I had fallen in love with from the moment I saw him standing in his banana briefs. Even back then, deep, *deep* down, I knew I had fallen for him. It was love at first sight, except I was too scared to even think about it.

Not now, though. I could see that what I felt was real and there was no reason to be scared anymore.

"Come on," I said, kissing him again. "Let's get cleaned up. We've got breakfast to go to."

"Breakfast? But I already ate," Shy said, giving my ass a

playful slap as I got up from the bed, come smeared across my chest and stomach.

"Well, make room for some more sausage and eggs." I grabbed a hand towel from the bathroom and threw one to Shiro, who wiped himself off and met me inside the bathroom, still wearing that drunken smile. I couldn't help but kiss him again. Distance had sucked, but it wasn't anything we couldn't overcome. It just meant I had to cherish every moment we spent together that much more. And that meant showering Shy in as many kisses as I could manage.

Although, with the Christmas gift I planned on giving Shiro, I hoped the distance would become even less of an issue.

We hopped in the shower and washed each other off. After we avoided getting distracted once again, we went to change into our clothes.

"Wait, hold on," Shiro said before I took off my towel and pulled on my briefs. "I've got a Christmas gift for you. Nothing major, but, well I couldn't help it."

He went over to his suitcase and unzipped it. He pulled out a wrapped box, the silver wrapping paper crinkling as he brought it over to me. I smiled and gave him a kiss as thanks.

"You really didn't have to." I knew how difficult it could be trying to find a gift for someone who had almost everything he could ask for, so I appreciated even just the thought. But when I opened the black box underneath the wrapping, I appreciated the gift even more.

"Like them?" Shy asked as I pulled the jockstraps out of the box, smiling wide.

"I love them," I said, checking out the pair of underwear. The box had brought two, one for Shy and one for me. They were both silky and black, with cartoon bananas printed across the thick white waistband.

"Now you can be banana boy, too." Shy kissed me as I thanked him again, absolutely loving my gift. I handed him his pair with another kiss. I couldn't stop.

"Let's start a tradition," I said, checking us out with our new jockstraps. Shy filled his out in a way that had my mouth watering. "Let's wear these every Christmas."

"Deal." Shy gave a playful grab at my growing bulge. "Now let's keep getting dressed so we don't miss breakfast."

"Hold on, hold on." It was my turn. I went over to my closet and opened it, reaching up to the top shelf, above the rack of coats. I grabbed the small rectangular box and walked back to Shy's side. "I was going to wait, but screw it —it already feels like I've been waiting my whole life." I handed over the box, wrapped in a royal blue wrapping with a red velvet bow tied around the center and across its length. "Open it."

He looked at me, eyes glittering, and he opened the gift, taking more care than I had with the ribbon and wrapping. He reached the long black box underneath it all. Behind him, on the windowsill, I could see a small accumulation of the snow that had fallen the night before. We didn't get it every holiday season, but it seemed like this year Spain had been especially cold, and the night before we had been given the gift of waking up to a white Christmas.

"Nick..." He opened the box and let out a surprised sound. "Nick!"

It was a key, golden and curved and heavy, its handle inscribed with delicate flowerlike filigree.

"It's the key to the palace," I said. "I want you to move here. I want you to spend as much time as you can here, and then for the months you have to go back to the US, then I'll travel back with you. I've spoken to my parents about it, and they think it's a great idea. You know how much my mom loves you, and my dad's excited to get to know you more, too."

We had already discussed some kind of arrangement where we saw each other for more than five days at a time, and this felt like the absolute best way to remedy that.

Judging by the look on Shy's face, he thought the same thing. "I'll have to figure out my job..."

"I've thought about that, too. I think you can pick up cases here. You're basically fluent in Spanish already, and you're damn good at your job. I think Spain could use you, especially the LGBTQ community. I've gotten so many emails, so many letters—you've read a few of them. There's so much pain out there, but there's also a lot of hope. I think you can give people that hope. We can get a working visa sorted and make your home base here, at the palace. I'd love to open up a section for LGBTQ activism, maybe have your agency also stationed here."

"My own agency... Jesus, Nick. That all sounds...that all sounds absolutely incredible." He almost seemed brought to tears. He set the box down on the dresser and wrapped me up into a tight hug. "I'm speechless," he said into my neck. "Really."

When he took a step back, I could tell he had been crying, his eyes shining.

"So you'll move in?"

"Yes, abso-fucking-lutely," he said with a laugh, wiping at his eyes.

"Good." And, *oncccee* again, I had to kiss him. "Merry Christmas, *mi amor.*"

"Merry Christmas, my prince."

We finished getting ready, both of us glowing as we hopped around the bedroom, as if there were a song playing even though it was silent.

Shy looked especially handsome in a green-and-blue cardigan my mom had given him as a gift, designed by Marques Molano, one of her absolute favorite designers. It fit him well, hugging his muscles and making his light brown eyes pop. His hair was gelled with a dry matte paste so that it rose up in the front while cut short on the sides. He looked like a holiday snack, and all I wanted to do was eat him up.

I checked myself out in the mirror next to him, finding us to be an attractive couple if I really allowed myself to gloat. I stood a few inches taller than him and seemed to complement him in every way, even in the red-and-white-striped cardigan I had thrown on. My hair had been cut short all around, although I let my beard grow in a little more than Shy's bare face. I looped a hand around his waist and smiled at the picture of us.

On Shy's wrist was a glittering golden bracelet—a gift from my father. It had been his father's, and he had given it to Shy after he'd spent two weeks with us, the two of them having formed a deep bond. I was proud of my father, who stood strong and supported me, even when the church was clawing at his back, throwing baseless threats at us. It had turned pretty nasty, but my father never turned his back on me or Shy. He accepted him into the family and was quickly becoming a very loud voice in support of the LGBTQ movement, especially in Spain where public perception was shifting at an incredible rate and in the right direction.

"Maybe we can wear this for the *People* magazine interview?" Shy said, cocking his head to the side as he considered it.

"I like it, but the wardrobe people will probably have something for us."

"Right, duh. Still have to get used to this."

"You're doing great," I said, grabbing his hand. And he really was doing great. When we went public through an interview with Oprah, we knew that our relationship would explode into every headline within hours. And, sure enough, we were the trending topic for months. It had been around seven months since the interview, and I still woke up to random days where our names were trending simply because we were photographed out in public together, smiling and laughing about some silly joke. That had never happened to me before. My name never used to trend for this long, and it never trended globally, that's for sure. I was used to the public eye, but I had to admit, I wasn't used to the intensity of the attention that came after I went public with my relationship and sexuality. Things went from zero to three hundred in seconds flat. I worried about Shy, especially in the earlier days when his Instagram account blew up from four hundred followers to one million followers in a matter of days. Suddenly, people were either lifting him up or tearing him apart, and the noise was coming from all different directions. It was enough to drive anyone crazy if they allowed it, if they sat and read through each and every comment, each and every retweet. He had been open about his worries with me, and thankfully, his head never got too big, nor did he ever dive into the dark depths of the comment sections on any of the articles covering us. He stayed himself through it all, a positive and bright and intelligent soul. He stayed as the man I had fallen so deeply in love with.

We left my bedroom and were immediately stopped, Shy letting out an excited "aww" and dropping to his knees.

"Eli," I said, scratching my dog's back as he showered Shy in morning licks. He had a plush evergreen velvet bed next to my door, in case he ever wandered over and the door was closed. We had found him sleeping outside the door on multiple occasions, and so I decided to have a bed placed next to it just in case.

Outside of the hall's arching windows, I could see the snow-blanketed grounds more clearly. It hadn't been a heavy snow, just enough to paint the landscape into a winter wonderland. I could see trails of footsteps cutting across where paths used to be, paws appearing where a cat must have crossed, leading up to a snow-covered oak tree.

I crouched back down and joined the cuddle puddle that formed between Eli and Shy, getting some dog kisses on my cheek, feeling like this truly was the most wonderful time of the year.

The End

Want to read an extra steamy scene with Ace, Rex, and their date for the night? Sign up for my mailing list and receive their scene plus a bonus story, WALK ON THE WILD SIDE, for free!

And be sure to connect with me on Instagram **@maxwalkerwrites** and in my private Facebook group: Mad for Max Walker.

Or send me an email at MaxWalkerAuthor@Outlook.com

THANK YOU

Thank you for reading A Royal Christmas Cruise! If you enjoyed this book, then consider reading my other Stonewall Investigations Christmas Story:

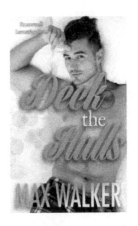

Free through Kindle Unlimited!

ALSO BY MAX WALKER

The Stonewall Investigation Series

A Hard Call

A Lethal Love

A Tangled Truth

A Lover's Game

The Stonewall Investigation Series - Miami

Bad Idea

Lie With Me

The Ace's Wild Series

Loosen Up

The Sierra View Series

Code Silver

Code Red

Code Blue

Code White

The Guardian Series

Books 1-4 Box Set

Audiobooks:

Christmas Stories: